A DEADLY
CHANGE OF LUCK

A DEADLY
CHANGE
OF LUCK

•

Gina Cresse

AVALON BOOKS
NEW YORK

PRINTED IN THE UNITED STATES OF AMERICA
ON ACID-FREE PAPER
BY HADDON CRAFTSMEN, BLOOMSBURG, PENNSYLVANIA

For everyone who's ever hoped for that elusive fortune
only achieved through fantastic luck.

Prologue

Lou Winnomore slapped the lottery ticket down on the counter, grinning from ear to ear. "You're lookin' at a winning ticket, right there," he bragged to Casey, the young grocery clerk standing behind the counter.

Casey eyed him suspiciously. "Yeah, right. Like last time when you won five bucks?"

"Better than that. Go ahead. Run it through your machine right there. You'll see," Lou insisted.

Casey wiped her hands on the green apron hung around her neck and shuffled over to the lottery machine. She accidentally bumped a display of key chains and knocked them on the floor. She set the ticket down on the counter and began picking up the key chains.

Lou wagged his head from side to side. "Get that later, Casey! Check the numbers first."

"Hey, Lou!" a man called as he appeared from the storeroom carrying a case of cat food. The man was as big as a fridge and carried himself like a professional wrestler, strutting down the aisle with his arms bulging under his shirt. He had a slight underbite and his eyes bulged a little, making him look like a bulldog. His bald head was freshly shaved and buffed to a sheen. He wore a green apron just like the one Casey had on.

"Morning, Otis," Lou said.

Otis noticed Casey huddled over the pile of key chains. He set the heavy box down. "Here, I'll get that, Casey. Go ahead and take care of Lou."

Casey straightened up, rolled her eyes and yawned as she slipped the ticket into the slot of the big green machine. She inspected the polish on her fingernails while she waited for the results to display. A number finally flashed on the screen. She glared at Lou.

"You won twenty-five bucks. Big deal. I could have finished picking up this mess," Casey complained. She opened the cash drawer and pulled out his prize money.

Otis hung the last key chain on the rack and frowned at Casey. "You better work on your customer relation skills, young lady."

Casey slammed the cash drawer closed and handed Lou his money. "Congratulations, Lou. Here's your twenty-five bucks. Don't spend it all in one place."

"Cheer up, Casey. You don't know how lucky you are, having a dad like Otis."

"You mean the dictator?"

Otis gently pulled a tuft of Casey's hair. "That's enough. Now, ring him up."

Lou set his grocery basket on the counter. "How's business?"

"Oh, I can't complain," Otis answered.

Casey rolled her eyes. She always reminded Lou of a pixie with great big green eyes and red hair cut short like a boy's. The top of her head barely came to her father's elbow, and Lou would have been surprised if she weighed more than ninety pounds. Her fingernails were chewed down to tiny pink stubs. She picked a can of beans out of Lou's basket, searched for the code and ran it across the scanner. Otis ignored her apparent irritation with him.

"How's retired life treating you?" Otis asked, pulling a feather duster out of his back pocket to knock down a cobweb that caught his attention.

"Oh, I don't know. Gets a little lonely, ever since Maggie passed away. Always thought we'd get to spend a few years together after I retired, you know, maybe travel a little."

Otis nodded as if he understood, but he didn't. He understood balance sheets and profit margins, but not feelings of loss and sadness.

Casey glanced at her father as she pulled a bottle of vitamins from Lou's basket. She was curious to see if he'd have any kind words for Lou. As she expected, he remained mute.

Lou felt Otis' discomfort and changed the subject. He'd spent so many months moping about Maggie's death and bringing people down that he felt like a boat anchor. He sensed that people wanted to run the other way when they saw him coming, afraid he'd start going on about how much he missed her. He forced a big smile from somewhere within. "Joey's taking me fishing tomorrow. Gonna be gone the whole weekend. Going up to Big Bear. One of those father-son bonding trips. Hear there's some pretty good fishing at the lake."

Otis smiled, relieved he didn't have to deal with any touchy-feely talk. "I pulled a ten-pound trout out of Big Bear Lake last summer," he boasted.

Casey placed the last of Lou's groceries in a paper bag. She grimaced at her father. "You did not. There's no such thing as a ten-pound trout. What a big liar you are."

"Hey!" Otis boomed, pointing his finger in Casey's face. "I've had about enough of your smart mouth. Don't you talk to me like that. You may be in college, but you still live under my roof, and you'll treat me with respect."

Casey shot him a curt smile as she removed the plastic shopping basket from the counter and stacked it with the others on the floor. She turned her attention to Lou. "That'll be twenty-six, eighty-seven," she announced, giving him the same plastic smile she'd just given her father.

Otis hoisted the heavy case off the counter and headed toward the pet-food aisle. "Good seeing you, Lou. Have fun fishing," he called over his shoulder as he disappeared behind a display of toilet paper that was stacked like a pyramid.

Lou handed Casey his lottery winnings and dug into his pocket for the additional $1.87. She held her hand out, waiting for the rest of the money. As he counted out the change, he placed an extra dollar bill on the counter.

"I almost forgot. I need to buy another ticket for tomorrow night's game."

Casey handed Lou his receipt and softened her expression. "You want to try a quick-pick this time?" she asked.

Lou shook his head. "You know I never leave chance to chance. I got my numbers right here," he said as he quickly selected six numbers from a lottery slip and pushed it across the counter toward her.

Casey slid the paper into a slot on the lottery machine and retrieved a ticket. "Good luck," she said, handing it to Lou.

Joey Winnomore pulled his pickup into his father's driveway at three o'clock on Saturday morning. He almost honked the horn to announce his arrival, but then remembered the hour and the sleeping neighbors. It didn't matter. Lou had been up and waiting for his son for nearly an hour. He peered out the window and spied the headlights in the yard. He rushed to the door, as excited as the first time his own father took him fishing so many decades ago. He hoisted a bag over his shoulder, grabbed his fishing pole and tackle box, locked the door and rushed down the steps, taking them two at a time.

Lou and Joey barely said two words to each other during the long drive to Big Bear. Lou sensed something was bothering Joey, but he didn't want to push. If Joey had a problem, he'd find a way to bring it up.

Lou directed from the dock as Joey backed the small fishing-boat trailer down the ramp into the lake. They loaded the aluminium boat with fishing gear and an ice-chest full of sandwiches and beer. After Joey parked the truck and trailer, the pair motored away from the boat dock, in search of the perfect fishing spot.

The little boat glided into a small cove on the opposite side of the lake. Joey cut the engine and dropped a small anchor over the side. "This looks like a pretty good spot," Lou said with approval.

Joey studied the landscape and nodded. "As good as any, I guess."

Worry lines appeared in Lou's forehead. Joey had lost a lot of weight lately, and he didn't have much weight to spare. His pants hung loose, and without the belt, would have slid right down his narrow hips. His shirt hadn't been laundered for weeks and was missing half the buttons. His face was gaunt and his brown hair was dull and unkempt. His dark eyes were usually alert and focused, but now they were bloodshot and heavy. Lou watched as his son reached into the ice-chest and retrieved a beer.

"It's seven in the morning," Lou reminded him.

Joey twisted the cap off the bottle and tossed it into the bottom of the boat. He took a large swig and wiped his sleeve across his unshaven face. "So it is. What difference does it make?"

Lou sat forward on the bench seat and looked his son square in the eye. "What's going on, Joey? You look like death warmed over. Is everything okay at work?"

Joey let out a cynical laugh and took another drink. "Everything's fine at work. Officer Winnomore never reports for duty under the influence, if that's what you're worried about."

"I'm worried about you, Joey. Tell me what's on your mind."

Joey reached into a paper sack next to his tackle box and pulled out a container of worms. "Fishing's on my mind. Want me to bait your hook?"

Lou studied his son's behavior. He knew better than to push. He grabbed his pole and picked the hook out of the cork handle. "No, I can manage," he said, picking a wriggling worm out of the container.

Over an hour passed before another word was spoken. Finally, Lou broke the silence. "You know, I won a little money in the lottery yesterday."

Joey barely reacted. "No kidding. Am I a rich man's son?"

"Nah. Twenty-five bucks. I always play the same numbers. I use the days from my kids' birthdays, your mother's birthday, and our anniversary."

Joey thought for a moment. "That's only five numbers. Where do you get the sixth?"

Lou smiled. "Scotty's birthday. He's my only grandson. Wish he could've come with us on this trip. Too bad he came down with the flu."

Joey stared at the red-and-white plastic float bobbing on the surface of the water. He squeezed his eyes shut for a moment, then took the last swallow from his third beer of the morning. "Scott's not sick. I just told you that so you wouldn't ask why I didn't bring him along."

Lou shifted in his seat. He sensed more to come, so he remained quiet and let his son build up the courage to speak the words he'd found so difficult to say. Both men stared out at the glassy surface of the lake. Finally, Joey opened his mouth.

"I'm in trouble, Dad. I don't know what to do."

"I'm listening," Lou encouraged.

"Me and Bridgett, we haven't been getting along too good lately."

Lou felt a twinge of relief. He and Maggie had worked through plenty of problems, but they always came through hard times with a stronger marriage and even more commitment to each other. This was something he could relate to, and maybe even provide some help. He'd felt so useless since Maggie died, but now he had something to offer. "Trouble with your marriage? You can work it out, son. I'm not saying it'll be easy, but—"

"You don't understand. We haven't been getting along for a long time. I'm afraid it may be too late to fix."

Lou put a hand on his son's shoulder. "It's never too late."

Joey reached for the ice-chest again, but Lou put his hand on top of it, preventing him from starting on another problem-numbing drink. Joey didn't fight him. He had no strength left to fight. He turned his eyes back toward the lake. "You were wrong, you know."

"About what?" Lou asked.

"About only having one grandchild. You're going to have another one in a couple months."

Surprised, Lou gave his son a confused look. "But I thought you just said—"

Joey's eyes met Lou's. In an instant, he understood. "Not Bridgett?"

Joey shook his head. "No. Someone else."

"Does Bridgett know?"

Tears began rolling down Joey's face. He couldn't speak. He just nodded.

Lou removed his fishing cap and began massaging the spot on his forehead where a pounding headache threatened to make the morning even worse. He had to fight the urge to grab his son by the collar and shake him violently. He wanted to know how he could do such a thing, but he also knew that being judgmental wouldn't solve any problems. He ran a few questions over in his mind: how could you be so stupid? What kind of an idiot are you? Didn't you think about the consequences? Then, he finally settled on a safe one. "What are you going to do?"

Joey wiped the tears from his face. "I don't know. Bridgett wants a divorce. She won't let me see Scott. She won't let me in the house. I'm gonna lose everything."

Lou nodded. "Probably. What about this other woman? Do you love her?"

"Love her? I barely even know her. She's a regular at that bar I told you about, where some of the guys from work hang out. She's giving me even more grief than Bridgett—making all kinds of threats if I don't do what she wants."

Lou combed his fingers through his gray hair then replaced his fishing hat. "What does she want?"

Joey stared blankly out at the surface of the water. A pair of ducks, leading a dozen fuzzy ducklings, swam past the boat. Joey wanted to smile at the sight, but he couldn't. "Everything I can't give her." Joey broke down and sobbed, his tears falling like raindrops on the floor of the boat. Lou sat next to him and searched for words that could help, but nothing came to him.

The weekend passed, and Lou and Joey managed to get through it with a few fleeting smiles and a string full of fish.

Joey dropped Lou off at his house late Sunday night. Before letting himself out of the pickup, Lou put a hand on Joey's shoulder. "Try not to worry too much, son. I know it doesn't seem like it right now, but everything will work itself out. You're gonna have to be strong. I'll be here for you, if you need anything. Okay?"

Joey gave his father a weak smile. "Thanks, Dad. You're about all I've got right now."

Lou watched the pickup drive slowly down the street, picked up the Sunday paper that had been tossed onto the front lawn, then he headed for his door. He patted his pockets, but couldn't find his keys. Eventually, he realized he'd left them on the kitchen table. In his excitement, he'd forgotten to pick them up. He reached as high as he could to the trim over the door and felt for his spare key. He'd locked himself out a few times over the years, and always kept a hide-a-key for just such emergencies.

He dropped his duffel bag on the back porch and left his fishing gear propped against the wall. He'd deal with putting everything away in the morning.

He'd spent the entire weekend worrying about Joey and still couldn't get his son's problems out of his mind. He plopped down in a chair at the kitchen table and rested his chin in his palms, staring out into space.

He glanced at the Sunday paper he'd placed on the table and reached for it. He knew there was no point in trying to go to sleep right away, so he opened it up and spread it out on the table. A story about a string of home invasion robberies in his neighborhood concerned him. He got up and checked that he'd locked the door after he came in. He returned to his paper, skipping over most of the stories since his eyes were beginning to get heavy and the words were starting to run together. He perked up when he turned to the section that reported the lottery results. He decided he'd check the numbers then go directly to bed.

Lou honestly didn't know why he bothered to buy lottery tickets. He'd convinced himself he was the unluckiest man in the world. He had a recurring dream that he was stranded in the middle of Death Valley with only one can of soda. When he opened the soda, a little speaker in the can would announce, "Congratulations, you have just won a million dollars," but of course, there was no soda in it. In his dream, he crawled across the sun-scorched desert searching for water, but never found it. The last scene from his dream was always of a pair of buzzards circling overhead as he took his last breath. He shook the unpleasant thought from his head.

He adjusted his glasses and squinted at the small numbers printed on the page. He rubbed his eyes and looked again. It couldn't be right. His mind was foggy, he told himself. He checked again. The first number was Frankie's birthday. The second was Nellie's, and the third was Joey's. The fourth matched Maggie's birthday and the fifth was their wedding anniversary. But what about the sixth mega number? Was it really Scotty's birthday? Could he be dreaming? He checked again.

There was no question.

He'd just picked all six numbers in the California Lottery, worth over $58 million. His heart raced and nearly pounded out of his chest.

The clock on the wall said it was nearly midnight. There was no one he could call at this hour to tell. He thought of calling Joey, but wasn't even sure where he was staying since his separation from Bridgett. He wanted to dance around his kitchen, but the dark cloud of Joey's bad news kept him from floating off the floor. He felt like an oaf for not asking Joey if he needed a place to stay. Lou would love to have his son's company. He'd been so lonely ever since . . . well, anyhow, he'd call Joey at work in the morning to tell him the good news. Then he could convince him to move back home into his old room until he got his life in order. They could cheer each other up just by keeping each other company.

Suddenly, he wasn't sleepy anymore. He walked around the house three times, wondering what to do. In the morning, he would call the lottery officials to find out how to claim the prizemoney. A sudden fear overtook him. He stared at the newspaper. Home invasion robberies in his neighborhood occurred every night for the past four nights. The homeowners were tied up and gagged while the robbers cleaned them out. Lou removed the lottery ticket from his wallet. He just knew that with his luck, tonight would be the night his house was hit, and they'd steal the ticket. He nervously paced the house, searching for the perfect hiding place until he could get it safely to the claims office to collect his winnings. He finally decided on a place he was sure no one would ever look. After he finished hiding it, he paced the house another half-dozen times.

"How am I ever gonna get to sleep?" he asked himself.

He wandered around the house, performing his routine chores in order to save time in the morning and, hopefully, to tire himself out so he could fall asleep. He poured himself a glass of milk, remembering something he'd read about how calcium could help relieve insomnia.

He grimaced at the price tag stuck to the lid of a bottle

of calcium supplements. Then he laughed. He couldn't believe he was getting all worked up about a few dollars when he was now worth over $50 million.

He danced around the kitchen and sang the name of every model car he intended to buy. Then he began naming cities where he'd like to have houses—one for every season. Then he remembered a yacht he'd seen in a magazine that he would love to have. He and Joey could go deep-sea fishing. He danced and laughed so hard the muscles in his stomach hurt and tears rolled down his face. He caught his reflection in the toaster on the counter and laughed at how red the distorted image of his face was. He looked like a clown.

He doubled over in the middle of his kitchen, wiping the tears from his eyes. He could barely catch his breath. Then, he felt a tremendous pressure around his upper torso. He felt like an elephant was sitting on his chest. He collapsed on the floor, clutching his shirt collar. His last conscious thought was that he really was the unluckiest man in the world. He'd just won $58 million and he was going to die of a heart attack before he could claim it. It was just like his Death Valley dream, only it wasn't a dream at all. It was very real and he was going to be very dead.

Chapter One

I had an appointment to meet Fiona Oliviera at her real
estate office early on Tuesday morning. Fiona was about
ten minutes late, so I waited in my car, listening to the
radio until she arrived. A classic rock radio station played
a little louder than someone my age should probably listen,
but I didn't care. I unconsciously tapped my foot to the
beat. The music took me back to the Seventies, when I was
a skinny teenager with nothing but horses on my mind.

My name is Devonie Lace-Matthews. I live in Del Mar,
California, with my husband, Dr. Craig Matthews. I made
a decision a few years ago that I didn't have the right temperament to have a boss or a customer, not because of any
specific aversion to them, but because I will nearly kill
myself to perform to their expectations—or my perception
of their expectations.

A minor heart attack and a stern order from my doctor
to do something about the stress in my life prompted me
to make a major life change. In order to maintain my health

and sanity, I dropped out of the rat race and opted for a simpler life. I quit my job as a database administrator for a major telecommunications company, sold my house, and lived on a sailboat for a while. Since I married Craig, I no longer live on the boat, but it is docked at our home and we enjoy it as often as we can. To earn a living, I search out bargains at auctions and probate sales and do my best to turn a profit.

I'd nearly lost track of time, singing along with an old favorite, when an older Lincoln Continental came barreling down the boulevard and swerved into the parking lot, nearly hitting me broadside. As it screeched to a halt, I wondered if I should just start my engine and go home.

The woman driving the car shoved the heavy door open, banging it against the wall of the building she had parked next to. She spent two minutes gathering armloads of folders and binders and her purse before she piled out of her car. I opened my door and stepped out.

"Are you Devonie?" she asked, flustered and out of breath.

I smiled. "Yes. And you're Fiona?"

"That's me. Fiona Oliviera. Come on inside," she said, dropping one of the binders on the ground, scattering the papers in all directions.

I began stepping on the sheets to keep them from flying away, then picked them up as quickly as I could.

"Thanks, toots," she said, as I handed her the crumpled stack of papers. She smiled, exposing a gap between her front teeth that a Popsicle stick could fit through.

Somehow, she managed to squeeze her size-ten body into size-eight Capri pants. It was a feat many women attempt, but not many achieve. She wore a low-cut tank top under a faded cotton work shirt that she tied snugly at her waist. I don't know why I thought I'd be meeting a professional woman in a conservative business suit when I made the appointment with her over the phone. She definitely was not what I expected.

She unlocked the door and I followed her into the Fiona Oliviera Realty office. She dropped her armload onto a desk and motioned for me to take a seat. She plopped down in a chair opposite me and began spreading papers out in front of her. I couldn't take my eyes off her hair. It was ash-brown and looked as though it had been curled with soda-pop cans, but not brushed out completely. Something else was wrong with it. Then I realized it was a wig, and it was slipping off to one side. She noticed my stare.

"What? Is it this crazy wig again?" she said, using both hands to smash it down on her head, wiggling it back and forth until it seemed to be centered more or less on her skull. In that process, I noticed she was missing six of her false fingernails. The four remaining were painted bright pink except where they were chipped at the tips.

I smiled, not sure what to say.

"How's that?" she asked, waiting for my approval.

"Better," I answered. "But, maybe just a little more to the left."

She adjusted it one more time before rifling through the mass of papers on her desk. Then, she took a pencil and slipped it under the wig, scratching her scalp. "I hate this darn thing. Itches like crazy," she complained, rubbing the pencil up and down, pushing the wig out of place, again.

"But I can't grow a decent head of hair since I turned sixty. Without it, I look like a radiation fallout victim."

I frowned. She seemed to be fighting the aging process with the determination of a Hollywood star desperate to remain young.

"But you couldn't give a hoot about that. You're here to see the bank repo," she continued. She put her pencil down and rearranged the stack of papers on her desk.

She stopped for a moment to answer her ringing phone. "Fiona Oliviera Realty. Fiona speaking.

"You're kidding.

"No. The people withdrew their offer last week. They got tired of waiting.

"Great. Fax it over. Thanks, Chuck."

Fiona hung up the phone, leaned over on her desk, and grinned as though she was about to reveal the secret whereabouts of Elvis Presley. "Toots, this is your lucky day."

"Really?"

"Yes. That was Chuck . . . oh, what's his last name?" Fiona snapped her fingers repeatedly as if the action would cause the man's last name to magically pop into her head. "Doesn't matter. He's the executor to an estate I've had listed for, let me see, must be almost six months now. Thought I had it sold, but the people got tired of waiting and found something else. It's a great deal. Better than the repo."

Fiona continued rummaging through the stack of papers on her desk, pulling one out to the top. "Here it is," she said, placing a black-and-white photocopy of an old house in front of me. "It's got potential, but it needs some TLC. That's tender loving care in real estate talk."

I nodded with understanding as I inspected the picture. The house was cute. It had a lot of curb appeal from what I could see from the photo.

"What it really means is the place is a wreck and after you've finished fixing everything that's wrong with it, you'll swear on a stack of home repair books that you'll never do it again."

I chuckled at her directness. "Is it that bad?"

"Let's just say it needs more than new paint and carpet. If you're handy at all, you can flip it and make a nice little profit."

I squinted at the photocopy in my hands. "Can you show it to me? I'd like to see what's involved."

Fiona smiled, revealing a thousand wrinkles on her over-tanned face. "Good. I had a feeling you weren't one of those gals afraid to break a nail or two. Let me get the key."

I rode with Fiona in her huge boat of a car. The springs on the old Lincoln felt like they hadn't been replaced since it was new, at least thirty years ago. She took the corners like a policeman in hot pursuit of a bank robber. I gripped the door handle and tried to remember that the car was built like a tank and could probably survive anything short of being broadsided by a truck.

"Come on, baby," she coaxed as she pressed her foot into the accelerator to climb a steep hill. We nearly ripped the door off a car as some poor unsuspecting man pushed it open into Fiona's lane. I cringed as she swerved to miss it at the last second, honking her horn as she blew by him.

"Another graduate from the moron school of driving. I didn't know you could get a driver's license from a box of Crackerjacks," she complained, leering at the man in her rear-view mirror. I shrunk down in my seat and peered into the side-view mirror, just in time to see the alarmed man shake his fist at us.

As we crested the hill, she pointed to a house on the right. "See that house? I just sold it last month. Cute little place, but the people who bought it—crazy as loons. Two bedrooms, one bath, and four kids—all girls. Can you imagine? Where are they all gonna sleep? Six people and one bathroom? The poor father will never see *that* room."

I shook my head, but before I could say anything, she was pointing to another house on the other side of the street. "Sold that one, too. And over there? That's my listing," she said, as the Lincoln drifted into the oncoming traffic lane. The car coming the other way blared its horn at her, causing her to swerve back to her own side of the road. She made the maneuver as though it were a common occurrence.

When we finally pulled to a stop in front of the little old estate-sale house, I peeled my fingers from around the door handle and rubbed them to try to get some blood flow back.

"This is it," she announced, pushing her door open to bang against a tree she'd parked too close to.

I eyed the house. "It doesn't look bad," I said, noticing that it appeared to be well maintained, except for the overgrown yard.

"The outside is fine. It's the inside that's the problem," Fiona explained.

I followed Fiona through the yard gate and up the path. The house was old, probably built in the Fifties, but it fit right in with the other mature homes in the neighborhood. It was painted Nantucket blue and white. Neat little shutters added charm to the front of the house, which would have been too boxy and plain otherwise. The gingerbread trim reminded me of visits to my grandma's house when I was a little girl. I half expected Grandma to greet us at the door in her apron.

At one time, there were flowers and shrubs in the flowerbeds, but they had died of neglect. A bougainvillea, displaying massive clumps of bright pinkish-red petals, flowed over the fence from the neighbor's yard. I could smell jasmine in the air. This would be a nice place for anyone to call home.

Fiona opened the front door, and I blinked a couple times to make sure my eyes weren't deceiving me. The scene was such a sharp contrast to the outside, that I couldn't believe it. Holes in the walls. Cupboard doors ripped off. Carpet torn up. Vent covers mangled and bent. It looked like someone had turned a herd of angry bulls loose inside the small house, then waved a red flag.

"What happened?" I muttered, gazing around the ruins.

"Vandals broke in. Darn shame. From the looks of the outside, it was probably a cute little place," Fiona explained.

"Vandals? Is this a bad neighborhood?" I asked. I knew that no matter how good the house was, if the area was bad, then I shouldn't waste my time or money.

"Not really. Oh, there was a rash of break-ins a few months back, but those turned out to be a couple of nuisance kids. Police caught them and scared some sense into them. Haven't had any trouble since."

I wandered through the kitchen, calculating in my head what repairs needed to be made—new appliances, new cabinet doors, patch and paint the walls. As I continued through the house, I couldn't figure what the vandals had in mind. It seemed almost as though they were looking for something, but I couldn't understand why they'd punch holes in the walls. Fiona followed me through the house, pointing out every positive feature she could.

"Now, close your eyes," she said, taking me by the hand to lead me out to the back yard. "This is the best part."

I obeyed her order and let her guide me through a doorway and out to a yard of overgrown grass and weeds. She put her hands on my shoulders and turned me until I was in just the right position. "Okay. Open your eyes."

I opened my eyes to a huge patch of bamboo that covered the entire back fence. It was at least eight-feet tall. "Bamboo?" I questioned.

"Not the bamboo. It's what's on the other side of the bamboo," she said, parting a clump of the overgrown greenery to give me a glimpse of the view.

I strained to see through the small opening she was able to provide. "Is that the ocean?"

"You know what that view is worth? Fix this place up, cut down these chopsticks, and you've got yourself a goldmine."

I pushed my way through the thick growth to the back

fence and brushed the tangle of leaves out of my face. "Wow. It's beautiful."

Fiona headed back toward the house. "Put some French doors here, a bay window over there, and voila, instant 'sells itself' charmer."

I followed Fiona back inside. This house seemed too good to be true. The asking price allowed more than enough for the repairs needed to make it marketable, plus a very nice profit. "What's the story on this place? Why hasn't some investor snatched it up?" I asked.

Fiona grinned at me. "Wait till you hear this story. You'll think it came right out of a bad soap opera."

"Really?" I said, waiting with anticipation for her to continue.

"You hungry? I'd kill for a breakfast burrito."

"I had breakfast, but if you—"

"Great. Come on. I know a great little place. My treat," she said, herding me through the house to the front door. I waited on the porch while she locked the door. "I'll tell you all about this place over breakfast."

I watched Fiona smother her scrambled-egg burrito with hot salsa while I sipped my grapefruit juice. She glanced around the restaurant coyly, then reached down and unbuttoned the top button of her pants. "These darn things are cutting me in half," she complained. "They build clothes for Barbie dolls, not for real women."

I smiled and nodded. I could probably tell her if she had salsa on her chin, or even if her wig was slipping, but I couldn't suggest that she buy a larger size, or even a style more appropriate for her age. Who's to say what women should wear, anyway? Right? But comfort should definitely be considered. "I found some great Capri pants over at the mall, and they're stretch. The most comfortable pants I own," I offered.

"Really? Stretch? I should try them. I can barely breath in these," she said. "So. What do you think about that little place?"

"I like it. You were going to tell me its story?" I reminded her.

"Right. You're the first one to see it since Chuck got things straightened out. It's gonna go fast. Thought about picking it up myself, but I'm too busy right now. Chuck's the executor, I think I told you. Previous owner died about five or six months ago."

"Heirs?" I asked.

"Plenty, but that's where it gets complicated. Man's wife was deceased. Had three kids—two sons and a daughter. Oldest son is committed to some institution somewhere. Locked him up after he wouldn't stop threatening to assassinate the president."

"President?"

"Of the United States. Don't remember which one. He's been in there twenty years or more."

"Oh, my. That's a long time. Guess he's not cured?"

"Not hardly. But his share will go into an account to help pay for his care. The daughter is in the Peace Corps somewhere in Africa. Took months to find her. She was notified but said she didn't want any part of the estate."

"What about the other son?"

"He committed suicide right after his father died. Real sad story."

I frowned. "No other heirs?"

"The son who killed himself—he was a policeman. He had a son with his wife—Bridgett was her name, I think. Anyhow, that boy stood to inherit his father's portion of the estate. But this is where it gets complicated. Mister Policeman had a mistress—Raven Covina was her name. She and Mister Policeman had an illegitimate son together. Named him Bahama Breeze. You believe that? Hanging a name like that on a poor kid? Some people shouldn't be allowed to reproduce. Anyhow, when Raven found out that Mister Policeman's legitimate son was going to inherit his father's share of the estate, Raven got herself a lawyer and demanded an equal share for young Bahama Breeze."

I shook my head. "I bet that didn't go over too well with Bridgett."

Fiona snickered. "Like a blimp full of bowling balls. That woman refused to sign any papers. She didn't care if her son didn't get anything—she was not going to raise one finger to help Bahama Breeze get a penny of that estate."

"So how'd you take care of it?" I asked.

"Chuck had to set up a legal guardianship for Bridgett's boy. Hired a lawyer. Ran notices in newspapers. What a mess. It's taken all these months to get everything in order so we could sell it. That call from Chuck was to let me know he finally had everything straightened out."

"There aren't any backup offers on it?"

"Well, we had a couple offers when it first came in, but the buyers got so disgusted with all the legal hangups, that they gave up. You just happened to be in the right place at the right time. I know Chuck will accept an offer close to the asking price. It's a real bargain."

Fiona drove us back to her office. My right leg felt a little weak from pressing on my imaginary brake pedal.

We resumed our positions at her desk, still cluttered with masses of paper.

"So?" she asked.

A fleeting thought raced through my mind that I should probably consult with my husband first, but I knew this place would not be on the market long, and I didn't want to risk losing it. Besides, this was my project and he trusts my judgment. "I'd like to make an offer, but it's a little shy of the asking price," I answered, confident that the house was a great buy even at full price.

"Super! Let's write it up," she said, rummaging through her desk drawer for an offer form. She snatched a pen from an old coffee cup that housed about twenty other pens and started scribbling.

Fiona skimmed over the paperwork she'd just filled out. I'm sure I initialed more paragraphs than are in the Constitution. I noticed the name of the deceased man on the paperwork—Lou Winnomore.

Fiona tried to call the offer in to Chuck while I waited, but there was no answer. She sent me home to wait.

I couldn't settle on any activity adequate to distract me from the anticipation of knowing if Chuck accepted my offer. "What did he say?" I blurted into the phone when the call finally came through. I knew from the caller ID screen that it was Fiona.

"When can you close?" she asked.

I smiled. "One week."

"Get down here and sign some more papers, girl. You just bought yourself a little goldmine."

Chapter Two

I drove my husband, Craig, by the house no less than five times while we waited for the escrow to close. I had affectionately named the place Rancho Costa Little. He was impressed with the deal I'd made, and was anxious to help me get started with the repairs.

He came home from his shift at the hospital to find me coloring yard-sale signs on the floor in the living room.

"Are we selling the yard?" he asked, kissing the top of my head as he passed through on his way to the bedroom.

"Yeah. What do you think we can get for it?" I replied, winking at him.

He continued down the hall, whistling a tune from *Snow White*.

"I picked up the key for Rancho Costa Little today," I called to him. "I ordered a big garbage bin from the sanitation company, too. They should deliver it next week."

He returned to the living room, still in his green hospital scrubs, with a stethoscope hanging around his neck and a tool belt around his waist. "Great. I'm ready. Let's go over there now."

I smiled at his enthusiasm. "Dinner's cooking. How about after we eat?"

He frowned, stroking the new hammer he'd bought for the occasion. "Okay," he said, sounding a little like a small boy who'd been told he can't have his pie until he's finished his spinach.

When we pulled into the driveway of Rancho Costa Little, the sun was already setting. Something caught my eye as we stepped out of the car. "Did you see that?" I asked, motioning toward the window facing the street.

"See what?" Craig asked.

I blinked my eyes. "I could have sworn I saw a light in that window. Must have been a reflection," I concluded. I shoved the car door closed and laced my arm around Craig's as we skipped up the walk to the front door. I slipped the key in the knob and turned it.

We both jumped at the sound of a thud coming from inside the house. "What was that?" I asked.

Craig moved me away from the door. "I don't know. Sounds like someone's in there," he whispered, slowly turning the knob and pushing the door open slightly. "Wait here," he said, taking a step into the house. I grabbed his belt loop and held him back.

"No way. Either you stay here with me, or I go in with you."

He paused. "You have your cellphone handy?"

"Yes," I answered.

"Good. Dial 9-1-1 and keep your finger on the send button."

We tiptoed quietly into the house. I left the front door wide open to allow us an escape route.

"Anyone in here? I'm armed, so you better not try anything," Craig called out.

Silence was the only reply.

I held on to his belt loop as we eased our way into the kitchen. I reached over and turned on a light. The place was even more of a mess than the first time I'd seen it.

"Someone was in here, but they must have gone out that way," I said, pointing toward an open window. The curtains were blowing in the breeze.

We slinked through the entire house, ready to either pounce or run if we came face-to-face with an intruder. The place was empty. Whoever had been there left when they heard our key in the door.

Craig and I returned to the kitchen and gazed at the mess. I grinned at him. "Armed? What would you have done if someone was in here and pulled a gun on us?"

Craig pulled a staple gun from his tool belt. "I'd a pointed this right between his eyes and said, 'I know what you're thinkin', punk. You're thinkin', did he just use his last staple to insulate the attic, or does he have a full load? And to tell you the truth, I forgot myself in all this excitement. But bein' this is a Black and Decker power stapler, the most powerful staple gun in the world, and it'll staple you clean to the floor, you could ask yourself a question. Do I feel lucky? Well, do ya, punk?' "

I giggled as I listened to his Dirty Harry impression.

"Seriously, you think we should call the police?" I asked, trying to keep a straight face.

"I don't know. What would we tell them? Someone broke in and messed the place up? We don't even know if anything was stolen."

"You're probably right, but if they broke that window to get in, we may need to file a report for an insurance claim," I reminded him.

We both walked to the open window to inspect it. "It looks okay," I said, sliding it closed and locking it.

"Maybe someone from the real estate office left it open," Craig speculated.

"Maybe," I replied, not convinced. I checked all the other windows in the house. None were open. Everything was locked up tight.

Craig and I returned to the kitchen. "That must be it," I said. "Someone left that window open and that's how he got in."

Craig found a box of large garbage bags heaped in a pile of old cereal boxes and canned goods on the floor. He pulled one out of the box and snapped it open. "Or some-one had a key," he offered.

"A key? But I got all the keys from Fiona. There aren't supposed to be any others."

"No one knows for sure. Maybe the previous owner gave a key to his neighbor. He's dead, right?"

"I would have thought—"

I was interrupted by the doorbell, then a shrill, "Hel-looooo . . . anyone here?" A couple appeared in the kitchen doorway. They were wearing matching Hawaiian shirts, Bermuda shorts, and bright-yellow thong sandals.

"Hello there," the man said, holding his hand out to Craig. He had long, white sideburns that disappeared under a skipper's cap that looked like it was a couple sizes too small. "I'm Bob. This is my wife, Agnes. We live next door. You the new owners?" He shook Craig's hand, then mine. I thought he was going to shake my arm right out of its socket.

"Hi. Yes. We just came over to start doing a little cleanup," I said. "I'm Devonie, and this is my husband, Craig."

Agnes briefly acknowledged me, then smiled coyly at Craig. Her white hair was pulled back in a loose bun. A pair of reading glasses hung from a silver chain around her neck. She clutched a small glass vase full of miniature daffodils in her hand. She held them out to Craig. "Here, these are for you. Sort of a welcome-to-the-neighborhood gift," she said, ignoring me altogether. I grinned. I sensed that Agnes had developed an instant crush on Craig.

Craig took the vase from her shaky hand. "Thank you, Agnes," he said. "But we aren't going to be living here. This is an investment for us."

Bob's chin hit the floor. His eyebrows nearly met at a deep crevice above the bridge of his nose. From the look on his face, you would have thought we'd just announced we were converting it into a halfway house for convicted criminals, or a chicken ranch. "You're not going to rent it out, are you?" he asked.

"No, no," I assured him. "We're going to fix it up and put it back on the market."

Bob let out a relieved sigh. "Had me worried there for a minute. Not a single renter on this block. All homeowners. Want to keep it that way. People take better care of a house they own. Pride, you know."

Craig patted Bob on the back. "Not to worry, Bob. We have no desire to become slum lords," he joked. Bob didn't smile. I don't think he found the humor in it.

"Thank you so much for the daffodils. They're one of my favorite flowers," I said, trying to launch the conversation in a new direction.

"I grew them myself," Agnes boasted, still ogling Craig. He has a quality that attracts women, like little girls to kittens. If I were a less secure wife, I'd probably be worried about all those pretty nurses he works with, but I trust him more than anyone in the world.

"Really?" he said, admiring the bouquet in his hand. "They're beautiful."

I cleared my throat. "On a completely different subject, did either of you see someone lurking around here earlier?"

"Lurking? You mean, like sneaking?" Bob asked.

"Yes. When we got here, someone was inside. When they heard us come in, they went out the window."

"My goodness," Agnes gasped. "Just like those hoodlums they caught a while back. Nasty creatures."

"Hoodlums?" I questioned.

"Kids. Tried to break into our place, but Tiger scared 'em off," Bob said.

"Tiger?" Craig asked.

"Yeah. He's our dog. Cocker Spaniel. Looks sweet as candy, but if he don't love you, he'd just as soon take your leg off," Bob said, chuckling.

"Great watchdog," I said. "Fiona told me about those kids. She said the police caught them?"

"That's right," Bob replied. "Two of 'em. Hauled 'em off in a police car late one night. Never bothered us again."

"Hmm. I wonder if they're back?" I said. "Maybe we should call the police."

"Probably be a good idea," Craig said. He pulled his cellphone out of his pocket. "I'll give them a call," he continued, excusing himself to another room.

"By the way," I said. "Were you friends of the previous owner?"

"Ol' Lou? Great guy," Bob said. "We had him over for dinner every week after his wife died. Poor fella. Thought he was gonna die of pure loneliness after she passed."

"That's too bad. You didn't happen to have a key to this house, did you?"

"A key? No. We did watch the place for him whenever he went away, but he didn't give us a key. He kept one over the door on the trim ledge. We just used that if we needed to bring in his mail or water his plants," Bob explained.

"A hide-a-key? I wonder if it's still there?" I said, walking to the door to check. I stepped out onto the porch and stretched my arm up over the door. It was too high for me to reach.

Bob, who was a good six inches taller than me, offered his assistance. "Here, let me get it," he said, feeling along the top of the trim. "Hmm. Not here." He wiped the dust from his hand on his loudly colored shirt.

"Fiona must have given it to me," I said, leading the way back into the kitchen. "Maybe I'll call her tomorrow to make sure. I'd hate to think some stranger out there has a key."

Craig returned to the kitchen, slipping his cellphone back in his pocket. "I made a report. They said they'd have a patrol car do some drivebys for a while."

"Lot of good that'll do," Bob complained. "They ought a set up a sniper on that back fence there. He could hide in all that bamboo. Take care of the problem once and for all."

Craig chuckled. "Maybe we should just borrow Tiger for a while. Sounds like he could do the job."

"Darn right. Any time you want him, I'll bring him over," Bob said, patting Agnes on the shoulder. "Come on, pumpkin. Let's let these kids get to work."

Agnes nodded. She reached out and took Craig's hand, patting it. "So nice to meet you," she told him, grinning like a little girl stroking her new pony. She let her eyes stop on me for a brief moment, then frowned. "You, too." She made it sound as if I were a poor little stepdaughter, kept around only to clean the chimney.

I stopped Bob on his way out the door. "If I give you our phone number, would you call us if you see any strangers hanging around the house?"

Bob nodded. "Sure. I'll even sic Tiger on 'em if they're up to no good."

I laughed and handed Bob a card with our number on it.

Bob and Agnes left us to our task of cleaning up the place. "Where do you want to start?" Craig asked.

I gazed around the kitchen. "Why don't we start here? I want to try to sell anything that's not broken, so let's put yard-sale items over in that corner. We can use these garbage bags for the rest of the stuff."

"Good idea. We can store the garbage in the garage until

the bin gets here," Craig said, picking up the remains of a broken plate and dropping it into a plastic bag.

After thirty minutes of sorting and tossing and lifting and wiping, I'd begun to work up a sweat. "Hey, honey. Could you switch that ceiling fan on? I think that's the switch there on the wall next to you."

Craig looked in the direction I was pointing. "Sure," he said, flipping the switch. I heard the faint hum of the fan motor as it began to turn slowly.

I fanned my damp face. "That's too slow. Let me see if I can speed it up," I said, reaching for the chain to change the speed. I pulled once, then twice before I felt an adequate flow of air. "That's better."

After about ten seconds, I noticed a tick-tick sound coming from the fan. I tried to ignore it, but it began to get annoying. I looked up at it to see the pull-chain knob swinging back and forth, clanging against the glass shades.

"It's out of balance," Craig explained. "Want me to turn it off?"

I shook my head. "I've heard you can tape a penny to the top of one of the blades to fix it."

"Ever try it?" Craig asked.

"No. Think it'll work?"

"I don't know. It's worth a try." Craig reached into his pocket and pulled out a penny. "Here. I've got some electrical tape in my tool belt."

I turned the fan off and moved a kitchen chair over to a spot under the fan and stood on it. "I wonder how I can tell which blade needs the extra weight?"

Craig handed me a piece of tape. "Trial and error. I'll work the switch if you work the penny."

"Okay." I reached over my head and felt the top of a fan blade. "Yuck. It's all dirty up here. I need to wipe it off or the tape won't stick."

"Here's a rag," Craig said, handing me a dish towel.

I wiped the dust off the first two fan blades. When I got to the third one, for some reason, it was fairly clean. "This one's not too bad. I wonder why?" I said, running my fingers along the top of the blade. I felt something stuck to it. "What's this?" I used my fingernails to peel the tape off the blade.

"What is it?" Craig asked.

I studied the small slip of paper. "It's a lottery ticket." I stepped off the chair so I could see it in better light.

"Lottery ticket? That's weird. Why would someone stick it to the fan?"

"I don't know. It's old. About six months."

"You don't suppose—" I started. Craig and I exchanged glances. We inspected it closer. I turned it over.

"Look. It's not signed or anything. It says tickets must be claimed in one-hundred-and-eighty days."

Craig calculated its age in his head and on his fingers. "We have five days left."

I handed him the ticket. "This is crazy. It's probably not even a winner."

"Right. Someone just taped it up there to . . . to . . . balance the fan." He flashed me an eager grin. "Come on. Let's check it out." He took me by the hand and led me toward the door.

We rushed home and logged onto a California State Lottery website. We searched for the numbers drawn for the day of our ticket. I felt my face go flush as I read the numbers. "Oh my God. Oh my God. Oh my God," I repeated as I fanned my face. Craig joined my chanting as we both danced circles around the room. The ticket was worth $58 million and we had only five days before it expired.

Chapter Three

Craig and I laid in bed staring at the ceiling. Neither of us could sleep. "Tell me again what we're supposed to do?" I asked.

"You already signed the ticket and made copies of both sides. In the morning, we'll take it to the lottery district office and fill out a claim form. After that, our job's gonna get hard."

"Hard?"

"Yeah. We'll have to decide how to spend it."

I smiled and glanced over at the clock. It was past one in the morning. I don't know why we even tried to go to sleep. "You know what I'm going to buy first?" I said, holding my hand up and staring at its silhouette in the faint light of the moon through the window.

Craig reached his hand up and laced his fingers with mine. "What?"

Before I could answer, we were both startled by the ringing of our phone. "Hospital?" I asked.

"Probably. I'll get it."

Craig picked up the phone. "This is Doctor Matthews."

I continued staring at the outline of my hand, dreaming of the days to come.

"Bob?" Craig said into the phone.

"No. It's okay."

"Yes, I'm a doctor, but that's not why you called. What's the matter?

"You did? Is he still there?

"No, no. Keep Tiger inside. I'll call the police.

"Okay. Thanks for the call. Bye."

I switched on a lamp. "What is it?" I asked.

"That was Bob. He said there's someone in the house," Craig said, punching more numbers into the phone.

"You're calling the police?"

"Yes. Then I think I should go over there."

I was already out of bed, looking for my jeans. "I'm going too," I announced. Craig frowned at me.

He finished his call to the police while I laced up my shoes. He pulled a clean shirt from the closet and started on the buttons. "Where'd you put the lottery ticket?" he asked.

"In the desk drawer," I answered.

"Locked?"

I nodded. "And I put the key back in its hiding place."

"Good. Let's go."

Craig drove us to Rancho Costa Little. All the way over, I kept thinking about the ticket.

"Don't you think it's weird that someone keeps breaking

into that house? It's not the kind of neighborhood for that. I think someone's looking for the lottery ticket," I said.

Craig gave me a worried look, but didn't answer. We parked in front of the house. A police cruiser met us at the driveway. An officer stepped out of the car.

"Did you report a break-in at this address?" he asked.

"Yes," Craig answered. "We don't live here. The neighbor called us at home. He said he saw lights moving around inside."

The officer studied the house from the sidewalk. "You have a key?"

"Yes," I said, handing it to him.

"Wait here. I'll check it out."

Craig and I waited in the driveway while the officer entered the house. A few minutes later, he returned.

"No one in there now, but the place is torn apart. You want to check to see if anything's missing?" he told us as he handed me the key.

"The place looked that way when we bought it," I explained. "I'm not sure I could tell you if anything was missing. This is the second time today that someone broke in."

"I didn't see any sign of a forced entry. All the windows are closed tight. Both doors were locked."

I looked at the key in my hand. "I think I'll have the locks changed first thing in the morning."

The officer opened his car door. "That's probably a good idea. I'll make a few drivebys tonight. Maybe we can catch the guy."

Craig and I inspected the house. It looked pretty much the way we left it—a mess. Before we left, I taped a note to the window of the back door. It read: DON'T BOTHER. IT'S NOT HERE ANYMORE.

Craig walked up behind me and read the note. "You think it'll keep him out?"

"I don't know. If he's after the ticket, he'll give up soon anyway. He's got to know the time limit is about up."

On the way home, we talked about having the locks changed on the house first thing in the morning. I told Craig I'd take care of it. Then we talked about taking a trip somewhere. Europe. Tahiti. Australia.

"You know where I'd like to go first?" I ventured.

"Italy?" Craig guessed.

"Wyoming."

"Wyoming? Why?"

"I've never seen Yellowstone. And after that, I'd like to go to Kentucky and watch the running of the Derby."

"The Kentucky Derby? That'd be fun," Craig agreed. "Then we should go to Nashville to visit the Grand Ole Opry."

I smiled. "I didn't know you liked country music. I'd love to go."

"I never told you I play the banjo?"

"You? Really?"

"Sure. People mistake me for Earl Scruggs all the time. Those guys who played "Dueling Banjos" in *Deliverance*? I almost got the part, only I was too cute."

I laughed. "You are too cute. Are you serious? Do you really play?"

"Yes," he insisted.

"Hmm." I smiled and eyed him sideways, wondering if

he was pulling my leg. "Where would we go after Nash-ville?"

"I've never been to New England in the fall."

"Oh, yes! I've always wanted to see the turning colors. And then maybe Niagara Falls," I continued.

"We could ride over them in a barrel."

"And then when we get out of the hospital, we could head over to Indianapolis for the Indy 500," I offered, with a straight face.

Craig smiled. "Grand Canyon?"

"For sure. I was there once as a kid, and what I remember most was how breathtaking it was."

"So it seems we could spend a lot of time getting acquainted with America before we head off to see the rest of the world," Craig said, as he turned onto our block.

"It would seem so," I said, noticing some strange lights in front of our house. "What's going on?" I wondered, straining to get a better look.

The red-and-blue flashing lights of a patrol car reflected on our windshield as we pulled into the driveway. Two uniformed officers milled around the front yard, shining high-powered flashlights behind shrubs and trees.

Craig and I quickly jumped out of our car. "What's going on?" Craig asked one of the policemen.

"Is this your house?" he replied.

"Yes. I'm Doctor Craig Matthews. This is my wife, De-vonie. What's the problem?"

"Your alarm went off. Security company couldn't reach you at home, so they dispatched us," the policeman explained.

"The alarm? Did someone break in?" I asked.

"Appears that way. Got a broken window at the back of the house. Is that your dog in the backyard?"

"Yes. That's Albert. He's big, but he hasn't got a mean bone in his body. The worst he would do to a burglar is annoy him to death by insisting he play fetch," I said.

The policeman laughed. "Yeah, he kept bringing me his tennis ball when I went back there. I called for backup. We're about ready to go inside to check it out—make sure no one's still in there."

I shivered. "You think someone is in our house?"

"Won't know till we check. You better stay over here out of the way till we're done," the officer said, leading us to a position behind his car. Another patrol car screeched to a halt in front of our house. I held on to Craig's arm and watched as two officers removed their guns from their holsters and entered our house.

Craig and I huddled behind the patrol car and waited. It seemed as though an eternity passed before the policemen came back outside.

"It's okay. No one inside," one of them finally assured us. "You folks should go in and see if anything's missing."

I walked close to Craig, clinging to his arm, as we entered the house. I braced myself for a tragic scene of broken glass and blank spaces where stereos and televisions used to be. I blinked my eyes. The house looked just as it did when we left, except of course for the broken window in the dining room. All the electronics were still in place. Computers exactly as we left them. Our emergency cash stash was still intact in the freezer, wrapped in foil. The little bit of jewelry I own was still tucked safely away in the velvet-lined box Craig gave me on Valentine's Day.

We returned to the room we call our home office. I made a visual inspection of the desk. Nothing seemed amiss. Craig and I exchanged worried glances as I reached for the drawer and pulled. It didn't budge. We both let out a sigh of relief.

"Still locked," I said, walking across the room to the bookshelf. I reached for the bookend high on a shelf and felt for the key we keep hidden underneath it. The key was still there—another wave of relief.

I slid the key into the lock and turned it. Then I slowly pulled the drawer open. My heart sank. Craig banged his fist on the desk. The ticket was gone.

"Wait, I said, rushing over to the bookcase against the back wall. I'd hidden the photocopy of the ticket in an encyclopedia. I ran my finger along the volumes until I reached the right one and yanked it off the shelf. I flipped through the pages. Nothing. I turned it over and shook it, but nothing fell out.

Craig watched, his face hopeful. "Are you sure that's the one you put it in?"

I nodded. "Yes. I put it in the L volume, for lottery."

"Are you positive? Maybe you put it under M for money, or T for ticket," Craig offered.

"No. I distinctly remember stuffing it in the pages between lottery and Lorenzo Lotto."

I plopped down in a chair and chewed on my thumbnail. This wasn't just a bad dream. The ticket was gone.

Chapter Four

Officer Graves was somewhat reluctant to include the missing $58 million lottery ticket in his report—especially since I couldn't produce any proof that it ever existed. Finally, after explaining to him how we'd found the ticket, and the multiple break-ins at the other house with nothing ever taken, he agreed that it sounded plausible, and noted it in his report.

"I signed the back of the ticket, so won't it be impossible for someone else to cash it in?" I asked.

Officer Graves stared at me blankly. "You should call the lottery people about that. I've never won a dime on the thing, so I couldn't tell you. But, I'm sure there's someone out there who can alter your signature enough to make it pass for something else, or even make it disappear—especially for that kind of money."

He noticed the gloom in my face. "We can try to get some prints off the desk, and that bookend where you hide the key."

"Don't forget the encyclopedia," Craig said.

Officer Graves nodded his acknowledgment. "If someone shows up and tries to claim the ticket, and if we can somehow convince a judge that we need fingerprints from that person, maybe you'll have a case."

My spirits lifted a little. Craig and I both gave samples of our own fingerprints so they could be ruled out of any prints they did find.

"Do you think we have a chance of getting the ticket back?" I asked Officer Graves.

He solemnly shook his head. "You've got a better chance of being struck by lightning than getting that ticket back."

My shoulders sank as I walked the officers to the door.

"Whoever has that ticket now is the owner. In a case like this, I'd venture to say that possession is nine-tenths of the law," Graves continued.

As I closed the door, Craig came up from behind and wrapped his arms around me. "Easy come, easy go," he whispered in my ear.

I smiled. "I'm okay. Less than six hours ago, I was perfectly happy. How about you?"

"Elated, as a matter of fact," he said.

"And now, nothing is any different than it was then. Right?"

"Right. Except for that broken window."

"Oh, yeah. Well, except for that. So we shouldn't feel bad that we were this close to that much money, and someone snatched it away. Right?"

"Right," he agreed, again. "Besides, it probably would have ruined our lives. I've heard that happens to a lot of people who win the lottery. They're miserable after a while."

"And we wouldn't want that, would we?"

"Never."

"Good. Then I'm glad it happened. I love our life just the way it is," I said.

"Besides, it's not like we're destitute. I mean, we can still go to Wyoming, and next year we can head for Kentucky."

"And after I make a fortune from the sale of Rancho Costa Little, I can buy you a banjo."

"That's right. And I can teach you to play the guitar, and we can start a little duo and play at birthdays and weddings, and we can sing—"

"Now I think you're really dreaming," I said, trying hard to laugh just to keep from crying. "Come on. I'm tired. Let's go to bed."

Who were we kidding? We'd just lost $58 million. There was no way I'd be able to sleep.

At six in the morning, I rolled over to see if Craig was awake yet. He wasn't, but I couldn't wait any longer for the alarm to go off. "How did they know exactly where the ticket was? And the key? And don't forget the copy in the encyclopedia. They must have watched me through the window or something."

"Hmm?" he mumbled, slowly blinking his eyes open.

"Last night. Whoever came in here knew exactly where to go to get the ticket. I bet the guy who we scared off yesterday waited outside and watched through the window. He probably saw us find the ticket, then followed us home."

Craig rubbed his eyes and yawned. "Could be."

"Then he watched me put the ticket in the desk and hide the key and the photocopy. Little pervert. I'm gonna start keeping the curtains closed at night."

"So you think he went back to the other house last night and caused a commotion just to get us out of the house?" Craig asked, stretching his arms over his head to wake up the muscles.

"Yes. But the question is, how did he know about the ticket in the first place?"

Craig pushed the covers off and rolled over to sit on the edge of the bed. He scratched his head and rubbed the stubble on his chin. "Good question, but it doesn't matter now. Right?"

"Right. But I'm still curious."

"Did you lay awake all night thinking about it?" he asked.

"Not all night. At some point, I fell asleep and dreamed we lived on our very own island. You built a hospital and played the banjo for all your patients. I was your nurse and wore a straw hat with the price tag still hanging over the side. I think I was missing a front tooth."

Craig laughed. "But I loved you anyway. Right?"

"I don't know. You only spoke German and I couldn't understand a word you said."

"Take my word for it. I loved you anyway. I've got to go to work. You're going to meet the locksmith at the house?"

"Right after the dining room window is fixed," I said.

"And you won't worry anymore about the ticket?"

"I'm not worried about the ticket. It's just that—"

"Good." He kissed me on the forehead and shuffled into the bathroom.

I stared at the ceiling. "Right, Devonie. Let it go," I said to myself. "Just let it go."

The locksmith finished changing the locks and handed me the new keys. I called Fiona to ask if she'd given me the key that Lou Winnomore kept hidden over his door. She never knew anything about the key. I was glad I had the locks changed.

I rolled up my sleeves and began sorting through the mess in the kitchen. I set a large garbage can in the center of the floor and started tossing anything that had no value into it. An assortment of glass and plastic vitamin bottles were scattered all over the countertop. I gathered them and set them upright. I started tossing them one by one into the can, but I stopped when I picked up a bottle that felt full. It was still sealed. I inspected the label. It was an unopened bottle of calcium—the same kind that I take.

"Hmm." I set the bottle aside. The safety seal was still intact, and it was far from its expiration date. I thought I'd take it home. No sense wasting it, considering the price.

I resumed tossing the other bottles. I picked up another bottle and shook it, as I had the others. It was empty. I noticed it was the same calcium as the one I'd set aside. I started to toss it into the can when I noticed the price sticker on the lid. I stopped and compared it to the other bottle. They were completely different. I sorted through the rest of the bottles on the counter. None had the same price as the new bottle. I picked through the garbage can and removed the bottles I'd thrown out until I found the one with a price sticker that matched the new bottle of calcium. It was on a bottle of vitamin E. The two bottles were the same size, and somehow the lids had gotten switched. I pondered the mixed up lids for a moment, then tossed them both in the can.

It didn't take long until the plastic bag in the trashcan was full. I tied it off and hauled the bag out to the garage. Three trashbags later, and I could finally see the kitchen floor.

I moved into the living room, dragging my garbage can behind me. Everything had been ripped from the walls except for a lone painting, still hanging perfectly level over the spot where the sofa used to sit, before it was overturned and ripped apart. The painting was a monotone landscape, done in all shades of purple. Dark mountains faded into pale lavender as they grew further away and blended in with the misty sky. A dark purple tree—almost black—stood in the foreground, drawing attention to its nearly leafless branches. I carefully removed it from the wall and leaned it against a floor lamp that was slated for the yard sale.

I'd just started working my way toward the first bedroom when I heard a loud knock on the front door. I opened it to find Fiona standing there, wearing a leopard-skin patterned jumpsuit, a big floppy sunhat, and rhinestone-studded sunglasses that came to sharp points at each side. Her wig still listed to one side under the big hat. She held a brown paper sack in one hand and a bottle of champagne in the other. "Hi, toots! I've come with lunch and booze!"

I laughed and stepped aside to let her in. I glanced at my watch. It was nearly noon. I'd lost track of time. "Come on in. Lunch sounds great, but I don't usually hit the booze until the sun goes down," I joked, leading her to the kitchen.

"The sparkly is for you and the hubby. Something I do for all my buyers," she explained, setting the bottle on the counter. "Hey, toots. This is looking terrific," she said, gazing around the freshly-cleaned kitchen. Her eyes stopped on the painting I'd just taken down. "Oh, I love that. The color is perfect for my living room. And that lamp is gorgeous," she went on.

"Your living room has some purple?" I asked.

"The carpet," she acknowledged. "And the walls. My sofa is lavender, to match the ceiling."

I tried to picture a room that was entirely purple. Somehow, it seemed to fit Fiona. I smiled as I collected the lamp and the painting. "They're yours," I said, standing them both near the door where she wouldn't forget them.

"What a sweetheart. Sure I can't pay you for them?"

"No. I was just going to put them in a yard sale. You're doing me a favor by taking them off my hands," I insisted.

"Well, this is turning out to me my lucky day. I was just gonna stop by to see how you're doing with the place, and I figured you're one of those gals who *forgets* to eat. Now me? I could never forget something so dear to my heart and stomach. But skinny little you? Anyhow, I figure you for a turkey-on-whole-wheat girl. Am I right?"

I nodded. "Perfect. Let's sit out back on the patio. I'll wipe off the old table and chairs out there."

"Great," she said, following me out the back door. "And I also figured you for a cherry-lemonade girl. Sound okay?"

she continued, pulling bottles and sandwiches out of her bag.

"Just right. How'd you guess?"

"I'm a people person. I've worked with people for forty years. I've learned how to read them. I noticed the other day when I took you to breakfast, you made a funny little face whenever a waitress walked by with a greasy old plate of sausage or bacon."

"Really? I make a face?" I said.

"Oh, don't worry. It's very subtle. Probably nobody else would ever even notice. But, like I say, I'm a people person. Sort of like a sixth sense with me."

I took a bite of my sandwich and washed it down with a swig of lemonade. "You'll never in a million years guess what Craig and I found here last night."

Fiona studied my face and grinned. "Oh, I love a mystery. What'd you find?"

I leaned over the table closer to Fiona so I could speak softly. "A lottery ticket worth fifty-eight million dollars."

Fiona nearly choked on her sandwich. She coughed and hacked as I jumped to my feet to slap her on the back. "Are you okay?" I asked, patting her firmly between her shoulder blades.

She took small sips of her soda until she was finally able to speak. "You have got to be kidding me," she said, wiping the tears from her eyes.

"No. Really. Someone taped it to the top of a ceiling fan. We took it home and checked the numbers. It's a winner," I assured her.

"Well, what the heck are you doing here with a broom

and rubber gloves? I'd be out spending some of that dough, toots."

I frowned. "We had a slight problem."

Fiona's smile faded. "Problem? God, no. Tell me you didn't accidentally flush it down the toilet. Or your dog ate it?"

I shook my head. "It was stolen."

"Stolen? How? When?"

"Early this morning. Bob from next door called to tell us someone was in the house. We locked the ticket in our desk and hid the key, then came over here. When we got home, the ticket was gone," I explained.

"Oh my God," she gasped. "I thought this sort of thing only happens in the movies."

"Apparently, it happens in real life too."

"Who else did you tell about the ticket? Someone had to know about it."

I shook my head. "No one. We found it and came right home. We checked the numbers on the Internet. We didn't call anyone."

"So how did they know?" she asked.

"I think they followed us from here and watched me hide the ticket through our windows. That's the only logical explanation."

"But how did they know you had it in the first place?"

"That's a good question. My guess is they did the same thing—watched us through the windows here. Whoever has been breaking in here must be looking for the ticket. They'd probably been watching me the whole time."

"You did call the police, didn't you?"

"Yes."

"And?"

"They weren't too encouraging. They didn't find any fingerprints other than ours."

"So if someone shows up to claim the ticket?"

"It's our word against theirs. As they explained to us, possession is nine-tenths of the law."

"Well, doesn't that just frost your apple cart! There's got to be something you can do."

"I don't know what." I paused and watched a humming-bird dart from flower to flower on a trumpet vine that had crept over the fence from a neighboring yard. "Was there anyone who seemed very interested in the house when it first came on the market?"

"Well, sure. Like I say, I thought I had it sold a couple times, but they all backed out."

"What about other people who looked at it. Any of them want to see it more than once?" I asked.

Fiona searched her memory. "Let's see. I can't think of anyone. Like I said, most people were scared off by all the work it needed. I don't think anyone came back more than once."

I finished my sandwich and drank my last swallow of lemonade. "Well, it doesn't really matter anyhow. Craig and I talked about it. We were happy before we found the ticket, and we're still just as happy now."

"But to have come so close, and have it taken away like that. I'd be a little peeved. Heck, I'd be more than a little peeved, I'd be downright mad. I'd be boiling over. My wig would be frizzed from the steam coming out of my ears."

I chuckled at the thought of steam bellowing out of her ears. "Calm down, Fiona. It's only money."

"Only money? The last person I heard utter those words was pushing a beat-up old shopping cart down Main Street and living under the Harbor Street overpass."

Fiona and I finished lunch and she left me to work on my project. On her way out the door, she promised she'd help in the search for the culprit who stole the ticket, for a six percent commission, of course.

I'd made my way to the master bedroom, lugging the big garbage can behind me. I began sorting through the rubble. I got pretty good at tossing objects across the room and making rim shots into the trashcan. I picked up a blanket that was piled on the floor and uncovered a wrinkled calendar. It was one of Lowell Herrero's Cow Calendars. I sat down on the floor and smoothed the pages, smiling at the amusing pictures as I flipped through them. When I'd gotten to the December page, I started back at January, only this time I decided to read Lou Winnomore's entries. There weren't many—a couple of doctors' appointments, a scheduled tune-up for his car, a few birthdays, and an anniversary.

It looked like Lou didn't have a whole lot going on in his life—either that, or he had a terrific memory. Then I thought, no, if his memory was that good, he wouldn't need to mark down the birthdays of his family members or his own wedding anniversary. I studied his entries again. Something nagged at me as I scanned the pages, but I couldn't put my finger on it. I finally shook it off and tossed the calendar into the barrel. I had too much work to do. I couldn't afford to lose focus.

I'd worked up a decent sweat and could feel the perspi-

ration drip down my forehead. I'd just about finished cleaning out the bedroom, so I decided to take a little break. I
headed down the hall to the bathroom and ran the cold
water. I splashed it on my face, then realized I didn't have
a towel to dry off. I looked at my dripping face in the
mirror when it struck me—the entries in the calendar, that
is. I used the front of my shirt to dry my face and hands
and ran back to the bedroom.

I dumped the trash barrel out on the floor and dug
through it until I found the calendar. I quickly flipped
through the pages and noted the circled dates. "That's it!"
I said. The dates that were most important to Lou were the
same numbers he'd played on his winning lottery ticket.
That made sense to me. A lot of people use special dates
for their lottery picks. I felt relieved that I'd solved that
nagging question, much like when I finally remember
someone's name, two days after I swore it was on the tip
of my tongue.

I began throwing everything back in the trash barrel, but
I still had an uneasy feeling. People who play special numbers tend to always play those numbers. Lou probably
played the same numbers every time he bought a ticket. I
wondered how often he played the lottery. I also wondered
who else knew about Lou's special numbers. I decided not
to throw out the calendar.

I returned to the kitchen and pulled my phone from my
purse. I called Fiona's office.

"Fiona? This is Devonie. Do you know how Lou Winnomore died?"

"Winnomore?" she replied, puzzled.

"Yes. The previous owner," I reminded her.

"Oh, him. Gee, toots, I don't know. He was old. I think his ticker just gave out on him."

"Heart attack?"

"I think that's what Chuck said, but you know I can't swear to it."

"So you don't know if an autopsy was done?" I asked.

"Autopsy? You may as well ask me what color the Queen of England's underwear is. I haven't got the foggiest idea, but Chuck would know," she offered.

"How is Chuck related to Lou?"

"Brother-in-law, I think. Yeah. Yeah. Lou was married to Chuck's wife's sister. They were twins. Not identical, but the other kind, you know, paternal?"

"Fraternal twins?"

"That's it. Fraternal," she said.

I studied the cow calendar on the counter. "Would it be okay if I called Chuck?"

"Sure, toots. I've got his number right here."

I dialed Chuck's number and waited for an answer. I used the excuse that I was cleaning up the place and found some photo albums, and wondered if any of the family members wanted them before I just threw them out. Chuck seemed like a nice man. He said that he didn't think any of Lou's kids would be interested in the albums, but if I wanted to bring them by his house, he'd take them. I could tell he didn't really want them either. He'd probably just toss them out. I told him I'd save him the trouble and do it myself. He didn't protest.

We chatted awhile, then I eased the conversation into the direction I really intended.

"Fiona tells me Lou died of a heart attack?"

"That's right," he verified.

"Gosh. That's too bad. Was he very old?" I asked.

"Not as old as me, but I've got old genes," he said, chuckling.

"Isn't it amazing what they can find out with an autopsy?" I said.

"Sure is, but they didn't do one on Lou. No reason to. He had a history of heart trouble. No one thought it was that serious, but Lou proved us wrong," Chuck explained.

"I see," I replied, still staring at the cow calendar I'd set on the counter.

I wrangled the conversation around to another subject and then gracefully let myself off the hook and said goodbye.

I headed for the garage and returned with one of the full garbage bags I'd put there earlier. I rummaged through two of them before I finally found the assorted bottles of vitamins and supplements I'd thrown out. I gathered them up and put them in a smaller paper sack.

I made sure all the doors were locked before I left the house, then I gathered up the bag of pills, the cow calendar, and headed for Detective Sam Wright's office. If my hunch was right, Lou Winnomore's cause of death was about as natural as my cousin Marilyn's platinum-blond hair.

Chapter Five

Detective Sam Wright scowled at me from across his desk. "Let me see if I've got this straight. You want me to tie up police lab resources to check out these pills because you think some old guy with a known heart condition didn't die the way a trained medical examiner said he did?"

I shook my head and rolled my eyes. "This is exactly the reaction I expected. I don't know why I even bothered coming to you in the first place," I complained.

"Because I'm the only fool here dumb enough to give you the time of day. Anybody else would throw you out."

I'd known Sam for several years. From the first time I met him, he'd shown a hostile tendency that still crops up from time to time. We're actually good friends now, but he still insists on making me prove myself every inch of the way when it comes to my conspiracy theories. I've learned to ignore his hostility, to a point. Once in a while, he follows through on a threat, so I've learned just how far

I can go with him. Most of the time, he puts up with my misadventures and comes up smelling like a rose.

"So, are you going to check out the pills?" I pressed.

"Tell me again why I should?"

I let out an exasperated sigh. "Because, as I've already explained, Lou Winnomore played his own special numbers. They're his family's birthdays and his anniversary. I'd bet you a hundred bucks he played those same numbers every time." I shoved the calendar closer to Sam and flipped through the pages, pointing out the circled dates. "The last ticket he played was a winner—fifty-eight million dollars. Someone had to know he played those numbers. No one could be that unlucky—to win fifty-eight million, then suddenly die of natural causes. Someone knew about the ticket, because his house was ransacked several times after he died. They were looking for the ticket. When I found it, they stole it from me."

Sam rocked in his chair and glared at me, but didn't say anything.

"And the lids to these bottles of vitamins were all mixed up," I continued.

"So?"

I crossed my arms over my chest and glared right back at him. "Do you take vitamins?" I asked.

"Yeah," he admitted.

"Do you take all the lids off at once to take them, or do you remove one at a time?"

"One at a time, but that doesn't mean—"

"Me too. One at a time. The only reason someone would remove all the lids at once is if they were tampering with them. They were probably nervous, and didn't pay attention to which lid went on which bottle," I speculated.

"That's a pretty far reach," Sam said.

"Far reach? So most murderers put the evidence right in your hand?"

He smirked at me but didn't reply. Typical Sam Wright. I reached across his desk and snatched up the calendar. I collected the bottles and dropped them back in the paper bag I'd brought them in. I jammed the calendar under my arm and grabbed the sack. "Fine. I'll go see someone else for help," I snapped.

Sam stood up and snatched the bag from me. "Don't bother someone else with your little escapade. I'll have the lab check it out, but if it comes up negative, like I know it will, will you drop it?"

I smiled. "Okay, but you're going to find something in that bag, and when you do, you'll owe me lunch."

Jason is an old friend of mine who owns an appliance sales and repair shop. He puts up with a lot more from me than a mere acquaintance would. I keep telling Craig that someday I want to throw a big "thank you" party for all the family and friends who've gotten mixed up in my capers. Jason would be at the top of the guest list. He got me a great deal on new appliances for the kitchen at Rancho Costa Little. I met him there early the next morning so he could install them. The top half of his body disappeared under the kitchen sink as he hooked up the new dishwasher. I sat on the floor to assist.

"Wrench?" he requested, holding a flattened palm out like a surgeon waiting for a scalpel.

"So what kind of poison do you think they'll find in those capsules?" I asked, placing the wrench in his hand.

The wrench disappeared under the sink and clanked on a hard-to-reach pipe. "Don't know. If you think he was killed for that lottery ticket, then your killer ought to show up in the next couple of days when he tries to claim the prizemoney," Jason said, between grunts.

"But if I can't prove Lou was murdered, then he'll get away with the money and the murder."

Jason held out his empty hand, again. "Screwdriver?"

I rummaged through the toolbox. "Phillips?"

"No. Flathead," he replied.

I placed it in his hand.

"Got any suspects?" Jason asked.

"No one in particular. Whoever it is probably knew him pretty well. He'd have to, to know the numbers that Lou always played. There are a couple of relatives who seem a little quirky."

"Quirky?"

"Yeah. There's a crazy son, but he's locked up in a mental institution," I said.

"You sure?"

"I was told he was." I wondered if Fiona might have been wrong about it. "Maybe I could call Chuck to make sure."

"Chuck?"

"He's Lou's brother-in-law. He was the executor to the estate."

"Maybe it's him."

"I thought of that, but decided he's probably not the one. He could have taken his time to look for the ticket before putting the house on the market. He didn't have to rip it apart. No one was pushing for the sale of the house."

"You're probably right. Who else?"

"A daughter. She's off in Africa somewhere. She's a missionary or something—has no interest in her father's estate."

"Probably not her then, either."

"Then there's the widow of Lou's third son. Now she's a possibility. Her late husband had an illegitimate son whose mother is demanding half of everything Lou's legitimate grandson gets for her own son. The wife doesn't want her son to have to share."

"Sounds kind of messy," Jason said.

"It is."

"But it could just as easily be the mistress, don't you think?"

I shook my head. "No. She wouldn't know anything about Lou, or the numbers he played in the lottery. I don't think it's her."

"You don't think Lou's son could have told her? Maybe she wanted to eliminate the middleman and get more money for herself. How'd the son die?"

"Suicide. I don't know the specifics. You think maybe she killed them both? Maybe she made the son's death look like a suicide and Lou's look like a heart attack?"

"That's a lot of maybes." Jason emerged from under the sink, his face contorted as if he were in pain. "I'm getting too old for this kind of work," he complained, rubbing his back.

I patted him on the shoulder. "Take a break. I brought a cooler of ice tea."

We sat at the table in the backyard and I poured the tea.

"So, it could be the daughter-in-law or the mistress. Any other suspects?" Jason asked.

I glanced toward the fence separating us from Agnes' and Bob's yard, and leaned closer to Jason. "Well, the neighbors were friends of Lou's, and they knew where he kept a spare key," I whispered.

Jason's eyes followed my glance.

"And, they were the ones who called us away from home when the ticket was stolen," I added.

"Really? How'd they get you out of your house?"

"They called to tell us someone was in this house."

"And you think they did that just to get you out of your house, then rushed over there and stole the ticket?"

"Maybe. All I know is, whoever did it will show up very soon to claim the prizemoney. All I have to do is prove that Lou was murdered, and the rest should be easy."

"Did Sam give you any idea how long it would take to check out the pills?"

"No. I'll call him later on to see if he's found anything yet. I wonder how long it would take to get Lou's body exhumed so an autopsy can be done?"

"Not before that lottery ticket expires, I'm sure. How many days left?"

"Three," I answered.

We were interrupted by Fiona's shrill voice as she called from the front door, which I had not locked.

"Yoohoo. Anyone home? Toots?"

"We're out back," I called to her. "That's Fiona. I asked her to stop by and give me her opinion on what I should do with that vinyl flooring in the kitchen."

Fiona appeared in the back doorway wearing black bell-bottom pants that were two sizes too small, three-inch platform shoes, and a red-and-white polka dot halter-top with a matching red blazer draped over her arm. The sight of her outfit sent me back thirty years to my youth, when hip-huggers and chokers were all the rage. I invited her to join us, even though I was sure she would not be able to sit down in those pants.

"Thanks, toots," she said, slowly lowering herself into a chair. I knew she was praying that the seams would not give way against the strain of her thighs. "I checked out that flooring on my way through the kitchen. Want my honest opinion?"

"That's why I asked you to come by," I said.

"Ceramic tile. It's not that hard to install, and it adds enough value to the house to make it worth the effort."

"That's what I thought, but I wanted to get it right from the horse's mouth. Bathrooms too?"

"Yes. And while you're at it, you might consider yanking that carpet out and putting something else down. The place is looking better and better."

"Things are moving right along. This is my friend, Jason. He's helping me out with the dishwasher and stove."

Fiona reached across the table to shake Jason's hand. I noticed she had ten brand new acrylic fingernails, painted bright red to match her outfit. "Well, you're a handsome thing, aren't you?" Fiona purred, stroking his hand with her fingers.

Jason blushed. I'd never seen his face turn that shade of red. I pretended to cough so I could cover my smile.

Fiona leaned over and whispered in my ear. "Does he know about the you-know-what?"

"The ticket?" I replied.

Fiona nodded.

"We were just talking about it."

Fiona grinned, exposing that big gap between her front teeth. "Good. I was glad you called me over. I did some checking after I talked to you last."

"Did you find out anything?"

"I went through my calendar. There was one man who looked at the place three times, but never made an offer."

"Is that unusual?" I asked.

Fiona shook her head. "I've had people look at a place five or six times and never make an offer. Buying a house is a big commitment."

I frowned. "We were just talking and I think finding out the *who* won't be as hard as proving that Lou was murdered."

Fiona gasped. "Murdered? Who says he was murdered?"

I'd forgotten that I hadn't spoken to Fiona since I found the calendar and the tampered bottles. I explained to her my discovery and filled her in on my theories.

"This is just like one of those murder mysteries you see on TV. What fun. So, how are you going to prove he was murdered?"

"An autopsy would have been nice, but once Sam comes up with poison in those capsules, I'm sure he can get a judge to order the body exhumed," I said.

Fiona's chin dropped to her chest. "Oh my God," she muttered.

Jason and I exchanged concerned glances. "What?" we asked in unison.

"Lou's body was cremated."

I had the same feeling I got when I realized I'd probably never get the lottery ticket back. Lou's body was gone. There'd be no physical evidence to prove he was poisoned. "Are you sure?" I asked.

Fiona nodded. She was adamant. "Yes. Chuck wanted to bury his ashes in the backyard—right over there," she said, pointing to a shady spot under a California pepper tree. "Can you imagine? Burying his brother-in-law in the back-yard like a family pet? I told him no way, of course."

"Cremated. I didn't count on that," I said.

The three of us stared blankly at the center of the table, wondering if our luck could get any worse.

Finally, Fiona shoved her chair back and stood up. "You're a bright girl, toots. My people-reading skills tell me you'll find a way."

I smiled weakly. Being bright doesn't automatically mean I have all the answers. Whenever someone tries to convince me I can achieve something because I'm bright, it usually turns out that my tenacity, hard-headedness, and strong will are the traits that get the task done. "Thanks, Fiona."

"I gotta go sell some real estate. Keep me posted on this. Okay?"

"I will."

Jason and I watched her teeter on those platform shoes all the way back to the house. I cringed, afraid she might fall and break an ankle on her way out.

"She's quite a piece of work," Jason commented, after she was out of earshot.

I smiled and nodded in agreement. "Yeah, but she's got a heart of gold."

Jason and I finished hooking up the range. At 11:50 my cellphone rang. It was Sam Wright.

"Where are you taking me to lunch?" he asked.

I chuckled with amusement. "Who says I'm taking you to lunch?"

I could hear him laughing on the other end of the line. "You did. You know those pills you wanted me to check out? Well guess what they were full of. Calcium citrate, magnesium, zinc, ascorbic acid—you want me to go on?"

"No way. That can't be."

"Yes, way. Little sister, you owe me lunch, and then some."

Chapter Six

I don't know what I was thinking. Of course the murderer would have gotten rid of the evidence the first time he broke into the house. He'd have removed any poisoned capsules that remained. The goal was to make Lou's death look natural. The situation was looking pretty grim. I had no poison. There was no body to autopsy. Sam thought my suspicions were unfounded.

I trudged back to the kitchen to continue helping Jason.

"Was that Sam?" he asked.

"Yeah," I grumbled.

"So? What did he find in the pills?"

"Nothing."

"Nothing? No poison?"

"No poison."

"Hmm. Guess that means you'll give it up now?"

I smirked at him. He knows me better than that. It takes more than a couple of setbacks to knock me off track. I dropped my cellphone back in my purse. "You ready to break for lunch?"

Jason chuckled. "That's what I figured. Too hard-headed for your own good."

I slung my purse over my shoulder. "You want lunch or not?"

"You buying?" he asked.

"Only if I get to pick the place."

"Okay, but I don't want any alfalfa sprouts or tofu. I want real meat and real sugar."

I slipped my sunglasses on. "How about white bread?"

"Yes. White bread, and lots of mayonnaise."

I headed for the door. "Come on, junk-food boy. Let's go clog some arteries."

I sat in the booth across from Jason, staring out the window at the parking lot. He sucked on a chocolate shake and waved his fingers in front of my face. Then he chanted, "Earth to Devonie. Earth to Devonie. Come in Devonie."

I snapped out of my trance. "I was just trying to think."

"But nothing happened?"

I ignored his joke. "How am I going to prove Lou was murdered? Sam won't help."

Jason slurped the last of his milkshake. "What about your suspects? Maybe you can tail them?"

"And then what?"

He shrugged his shoulders. "I don't know. I'm not a detective."

I stared out the window again. "Maybe I should wait till someone claims the ticket, then try to figure out how he did it."

"You think Sam would help then?"

I shook my head. "No. I'm sure I'll be on my own."

The waitress placed the bill in front of Jason. He slid it across the table to me. "What's left to do in the kitchen?" he asked.

"I want to move that old refrigerator out so I can put down the new flooring."

"You want to put it in the garage?"

"Yes, unless you want to try to sell it in your shop?"

"Nah. Too old. But I'll help you move it."

Jason brought in an appliance dolly from his truck while I tried to move the big refrigerator away from the wall. I could barely budge it.

"Here. Let me help," Jason offered, slipping the foot of the dolly under the huge fridge.

We struggled to get a strap wrapped around the avocado-green fridge. Finally, Jason was able to tip it back and move it out of the kitchen. I hurried ahead to the door that led to the garage and helped lower it down the concrete steps. We wrangled it into an out-of-the-way corner and left it there. Jason took the dolly back to his truck, and I returned to the kitchen with a broom to catch the dust-bunnies that had taken up residence under the fridge.

I jammed the broom into the corner, then stopped. A rectangular object caught my eye. I picked it up. It was a plastic pillbox—the kind that has the days of the week molded into the lid of each compartment. It rattled when I shook it. It wasn't empty.

Jason returned to the kitchen to see me shaking the box. "What's that?"

I opened the lids and grinned at him. "It's the proof I need. What do you want to bet?"

Jason stared down at the container in my hand. "Pills? What makes you think these are any different than the ones you already found?"

I snapped the lids closed and shoved the box in my purse, grabbing my keys at the same time. "I've just got a feeling. Could you lock the doors on your way out?" I called to Jason as I rushed out the front door.

Sam inspected the pillbox I'd placed in front of him on his desk. "Where'd you find it?"

"It had fallen off the kitchen counter between the refrigerator and the base cabinet."

He opened each compartment and looked inside.

"I got to thinking about those bottles I brought you. It makes sense now that if Lou Winnomore was murdered, the killer would get rid of any evidence he knew he'd left behind, but these must have accidentally fallen off the counter without the murderer knowing about it. Maybe Lou had some sort of seizure and that's when they fell."

Sam sniffed the opened compartments. I expected him to toss the box into the trashcan, but he didn't. He closed all the lids and dropped it into a small plastic bag. "Did you touch any of these?" he asked.

I shook my head.

"Come on," he said, launching himself out of his chair and marching toward the door.

I gathered up my purse and trotted after him. "Where are we going?"

"Lab."

"Lab? Really? What do you think it is?"

He didn't answer me. He just continued marching faster down the hall. I had to jog to keep up with him.

Eric, one of the police lab technicians, peered over his thick glasses when Sam and I entered the room. He was very tall, way over six feet. The sleeves on his white lab coat were three inches too short. He was very slim, and had curly blond hair. He reminded me of a big Q-tip swab wearing horn-rimmed glasses. "Hey, Sam. What's up?" he asked.

Sam dropped the plastic bag containing the pillbox on his desk. "I need you to check this out."

"Okay. Tuesday soon enough?"

Sam shook his head. "Now. I think we've got something here."

Eric frowned. "What are you thinking?" he asked as he slipped on a fresh pair of latex gloves.

Sam pointed at the pillbox. "Take a whiff."

Eric flipped open a compartment and held it near his nose. He eyed Sam.

"Faint bitter almond. You catch it?" Sam said.

Eric nodded. "Cyanide. This related to those vitamins you brought me?"

Sam nodded. "Found these after the fact."

Eric removed one of the capsules with a pair of tweezers and inspected it closely. "This is strange," he commented.

"What?" I asked, curious.

"These specs." He opened the capsule and poured the contents out onto a glass plate, then slid it under a microscope. He lowered his face to the eyepiece and studied the powder. "Check this out."

I started for the microscope, but Sam elbowed me out of the way. He looked through the eyepiece. "What are those dark specs?"

Eric shook his head. "Can't tell just yet. We'll run some tests and tell you exactly what's in those capsules, but it'll take a little time."

"Today?" Sam asked.

"No promises."

Sam stood up straight and scowled at Eric. I used the opportunity to peer into the microscope.

"I'll try, Sam," Eric promised.

I stared at the tiny specs mixed in with the white powder under the microscope. "Some of the specs are red, and some are blue," I commented.

"Very good. You know your colors," Sam said, sarcastically. He took me by the arm and pulled me toward the door.

"Eric, I need an answer today. Call me on my cell if you can't reach me in my office."

Eric frowned and nodded, returning to the work of identifying the contents of the capsules.

Sam marched me down the hall and out of the building. "Just how many people have you talked to about this?" he demanded.

I pulled my arm out of his grip. "About what? The ticket?"

"Yes, and the pills."

"Well, let me see. Craig, of course. And Jason, and Fiona."

"Fiona?"

"She's the real estate broker who sold me the house. You might want to talk to her. She knows a little about Lou Winnomore's family history. Real interesting stuff."

Sam scribbled something in his little black notebook. "Listen. I don't want a single word breathed about what we just found out. Got it?"

"Yes. Why?"

"You said that ticket expires in two days?"

I nodded.

"I don't want the killer to have any clue that we're on to the fact that Lou Winnomore was murdered. I want him to prance right up to that lottery office and wave the ticket in their faces."

"Can I tell Craig?" I asked.

"No one. Not Craig. Not Jason. Not even your houseplants. Understood?"

"Understood. But Craig wouldn't—"

"No!"

"Alright. Don't get so mad. I was just asking."

"Right now, I want you to take me to the house. I want to have a look around."

"Okay. Don't you want to have your team go over it? There's a lot of stuff there."

Sam shook his head. "I don't want a bunch of cops milling around the place. That might scare our guy off."

When we pulled up to Rancho Costa Little, a large garbage bin was parked in front of the house at the curb. I pulled into the driveway.

"Good. The bin is here," I commented.

"Don't throw anything away until I say you can," Sam instructed.

I calculated the cost of the bin on a per-day basis in my head and hoped he wouldn't make me wait months to use it.

I took Sam through the house and showed him where I found the few pieces of evidence that he'd already seen.

"Where's that calendar?" he asked.

"At home. I'll bring it to your office later," I said.

"Good. Where'd you find the pillbox?"

"Over here," I said, pointing to the spot on the floor.

Sam studied the kitchen area, then wandered through the rest of the house. "What's all this stuff?" he asked, staring at a bunch of items piled in the corner.

"That's slated for a yard sale, just as soon as I sort through the rest of the house."

"No yard sale until—"

"I know. Until you tell me I can. I'm not stupid."

He grunted what I assumed was an agreement to my remark.

I took him out to the garage and showed him the plastic garbage bags I'd already filled. He opened them one by one and rummaged through the contents. I sat down on the cold cement floor and watched him study the stuff I'd declared trash.

After he finished sorting through the garbage bags, we spent hours going through all the rooms of the house. We were interrupted when his cellphone rang out a vaguely familiar tune.

"Dragnet?" I asked as he reached in his pocket for his cellphone.

He grinned and nodded. "Wright here," he announced into the phone.

"Eric. What've you got?

"That's okay. Just tell me what you do know.

"So it is cyanide. Potassium?

"Sodium. Great. Thanks, Eric. Let me know when you get the rest. I owe you one."

Sam slipped his phone back in his pocket. "That was Eric. The capsules were filled with sodium cyanide. The guy was probably dead anywhere from one to ten minutes after he swallowed them."

I felt a little queasy just thinking about it. "Were there any fingerprints on the capsules?"

"You kidding? You wear rubber gloves when you handle cyanide or you die. It's absorbed through the skin."

"What about those specs? What were they?"

"He didn't have any results on that, yet. Thought he might in a half hour or so. I'm about done here. Let's head back over to the lab. Maybe by the time we get there, he'll have an answer for us."

Eric placed an art supply catalog on the desk in front of Sam. He leafed through the pages until he found what he was looking for. He jabbed his long, bony finger on the page. "Right there. That's what your little specs are."

I squinted to see the fine print. Sam moved Eric's finger out of the way.

"Dry art pigments?" Sam asked.

Eric smiled proudly. "Had a feeling that's what we were looking at, but I wanted to make sure. Cadmium deep red and cobalt blue, to be exact. Probably even made by this same company. They're the largest supplier in the country."

I scratched my head, puzzled. "Why would someone mix paint with cyanide?"

Eric crossed his arms over his chest and sat on the edge of the desk. "I doubt someone meant to mix them. The minute amount of paint indicates that it was merely residue. The guy probably accidentally contaminated the cyanide with a tool he used for multiple applications."

I read the description from the catalog. Dry pigments are used by some artists to make their own paints and pastels. They can be mixed with a variety of binder mediums, such as oil, watercolor, egg tempera, and gouache, whatever that is.

"Apparently, the guy isn't a stickler for cleaning up between projects. He probably contaminated his cadmium deep red with his cobalt blue," Eric offered, half joking.

I snapped my fingers. "Not necessarily." I jumped to my feet and grabbed Sam's arm. "Come on," I said, dragging him toward the door.

"What is it?" he insisted, balking at the door.

"Red and blue. They make purple," I replied.

"Purple?"

"Yes. Purple. Now would you come on?"

Chapter Seven

Fiona's office was closed when I tried to call her. It took me twenty minutes to find her home number on a card she'd given me, which I thought I'd stashed in a safe place in my glove compartment. When I finally found it and called her, she was anxious to have me come over to see her house. I explained to Sam about the purple painting I'd given to her on the way.

"Do we know who painted it?" he asked as I rang the doorbell.

"No, but maybe we can find out."

Fiona opened the door wearing a hot-pink satin robe. She wore matching high-heeled slippers with tufts of fluffy feathers on top. "Come on in, toots. I was just in the pool when you called. You bring your suits?"

"Not this time. Fiona, this is Sam Wright. He's a detective with the San Diego police."

Fiona's eyes strolled up and down Sam's tall body. For a moment, I thought she was going to leap in his arms and smother him with lipstick kisses. She reached out a hand to shake his, and the other she used to feel the muscles in his left arm. "Oh my, Devonie. You are just surrounded by gorgeous men, aren't you?"

Sam coughed and cleared his throat, pulling his hand back before she had a chance to nibble it. I'd never seen anyone intimidate Sam. I found it quite humorous that a little old lady could frighten this tough guy, even if she was acting half her age.

"Now what's this about my painting?" she asked, leading us toward her living room.

"I'm really sorry about this, Fiona. We need to take the painting to the police lab. It could be evidence," I explained.

"Margarita?" she drawled, picking up a pitcher of frosty-red liquid. "It's strawberry," she coaxed.

Sam and I both declined, although it looked really tempting.

Fiona replaced the pitcher on the counter. "Evidence?"

"I'm sorry. We really can't tell you any more than that," Sam explained. "Can you please give us the painting?"

Fiona's smile grew to a mischievous grin. "Why, certainly, sugar. I haven't had a chance to hang it up, yet. It's right over here, in my bedroom, darlin'. Why don't you come with me to get it? You're such a big, strong man."

Sam looked to me, as if I could offer some sort of protection from Fiona, who'd turned into a barracuda the instant she laid eyes on Sam. I sat down on the sofa. "You go ahead. I'll wait here," I said, picking up a magazine from the coffee table.

"Put that down. We won't be that long," he ordered, following Fiona down the hall.

Moments later, they were back in the living room. Sam carried the large, awkward painting while Fiona insisted on leading him by the arm.

"Come on. Let's get this to the lab," he said, rushing toward the door.

"Sure you two can't stay for a while? I could fire up the barbeque," Fiona offered.

Sam was already out the door and halfway to the curb. "Not this time, Fiona. Thanks for the offer, though," I called to her as I tried to catch up with Sam.

As we pulled away from the curb, Sam gave a nervous glance over his shoulder toward Fiona's house. "Why didn't you warn me about her?"

"Honestly, I didn't know you'd make such an impression. Come to think of it, she reacted nearly the same way when she met Jason. I think she just really likes men."

"If you haven't noticed, she's old enough to be my mother."

"That wouldn't stop a man if the tables were turned," I said.

Sam shifted uneasily in his seat. "Just get us to the lab. We're running out of time."

Eric scraped a few samples of paint from several sections of the canvas and examined them under his microscope. "Definitely the same pigment," he finally announced, after several minutes of whistling the theme song to "The Andy Griffith Show." "You know who painted it?"

I studied the lower portion for a signature. "Maybe

there's a signature under the mat board. Let's get it out of the frame."

We carefully removed the painting from the frame and lifted the mat board away. There was no signature.

"What kind of artist doesn't sign his painting?" I said.

"Someone who doesn't want to be sued. This painting is a copy of another artist's original work. I have a smaller print of it at home," Eric said.

Sam shook his head. "How do you like that? The guy doesn't have a problem with murder, but draws the line at copyright infringement."

Sam made a few notes in his notebook, then headed for the door. "Come on, Dev. I want to get that cow calendar— we'll need it for evidence."

Fiona called me on my cellphone while we were driving from the lab to my house.

"Did you hear the news?" she asked.

"What news?"

"The ticket. Someone claimed the fifty-eight million. Turn on your TV," she said.

"I can't. I'm in the car. Who was it?"

"Oh, toots. It's unbelievable. I know him! Can you imagine? He's a land developer. And here's the best part—he's not married."

"That's great, Fiona. What's his name?"

"Arthur Simon. He built the Simon Homes development, over by the mall. Beautiful homes, but that silly man—it's dreadfully obvious he hasn't got a wife—doesn't know what size a walk-in closet should be."

"Do you know where he lives?" I asked.

She hesitated. "Uh, let me think. Oh! How does this sound? Fiona Simon. Doesn't really roll off the tongue, does it? I wonder if I made the 'o' long—then it could sound French. Fiona Simone. That could work."

"Fiona. Concentrate. Where does he live?" I persisted.

"Oh, sorry toots. I tend to get a little carried away. I heard he has a great big house right on the beach. You know, I think I went out on a date with him once about twenty years ago. He came to pick me up wearing work boots. Took me to a pizza place. I got all dressed up and shaved my legs for pizza. Needless to say, there was no second date. Of course, now I could kick myself. He's one of the more successful builders in the area."

"Fiona. His address?"

"Oh. Right. You know, I don't know where he lives, but I'm going to find out."

"Fiona, he could be a murderer. You should probably stay away from him."

"But it's not a sure thing, right? Remember that old adage, innocent until proven guilty? As long as he's innocent, there's no harm letting him spend a little money on me, right? Or maybe I can sell him something."

"I'm hanging up now, Fiona. Be careful."

I dropped my cellphone on the seat next to me. "That was Fiona," I said to Sam. "Arthur Simon just showed up with the lottery ticket to claim the money."

"Arthur Simon, the builder?" he replied.

"That's what Fiona said." I pulled into our driveway. "Let's go in and turn on the news."

Craig was already home and had the evening news on when we walked in the door. "Hey, honey. You see the news? Art Simon turned in the ticket," he said, pointing at the television.

"Yeah. We just heard on the way over," I said.

"We? Oh, hi Sam. So, you ready to go arrest the guy?"

Sam was too busy watching the news to pay attention to our conversation. He pulled a chair closer to the television and furiously scribbled notes in his little book. Craig and I watched him like we watch the orangutans at the zoo—with amusement and fascination.

News cameras caught up with Arthur Simon and dogged him all the way to his truck. He seemed to be walking on air. He was an older, good-looking man in Levis and a work shirt. He wore a ball cap with a Simon Construction logo embroidered across the front. He was still wearing leather work boots. He looked like a man actively involved in the day-to-day workings of his company. When asked why he waited so long to claim the prize, he just grinned at the camera and said, "Sorry. I can't talk right now. I have a vacation to plan."

Sam jumped to his feet. "Like heck you're going on any vacation," he barked at the television. "I had a feeling this would happen. You got that calendar?" he asked me.

"I'll get it," I said.

"Good, then you need to take me back to the station so I can get my car."

I dropped Sam at the police station. As expected, he would not let me tag along to go talk to Arthur Simon.

The next morning, I cornered Sam in his office. "So? Did you arrest him?" I asked.

"Not yet. Not enough evidence," he replied.

"Not enough evidence? What about the ticket? How'd he explain how he got it?" I pressed.

"He said he bought it from someone yesterday for one million dollars—cash."

"What? Who'd he buy it from?"

"He didn't know. He never saw the guy. The whole deal was done with anonymous e-mail and a tricky exchange that required no personal contact."

"You're telling me the guy handed over a million dollars in cash to someone he never spoke to or saw?" I marveled.

"That's what he claims."

"And you believe him? Who in his right mind would pay for something without seeing it first? For all he knew, it could have been a phony ticket," I said.

"I never said he paid for it first. His story is that this anonymous e-mailer, who knew Simon could come up with the cash right away, approached him. Simon also has a reputation for being an honest, straightforward guy. I don't know if I'd agree after this escapade, but that's the image he has. He was instructed to go to the bus station. A locker key was stuck to the underside of a particular seat. He was given explicit directions. Inside the locker he found the ticket. He'd brought along a so-called expert to examine the ticket to make sure it was the real McCoy. When he was satisfied with the ticket, he placed a backpack full of cash in the locker and replaced the key under the original seat."

"So how'd the guy know he didn't put a bag full of newspaper in the locker? No one's reputation is that spotless," I said.

"Wait. I'm not finished. After he put the key back, he was instructed to go to the men's restroom and wait exactly five minutes. He'd been assured that he was being watched, and would not be allowed to leave the building if he'd tried to pull something. So he waited his five minutes, knowing full well that he'd given the guy exactly what he wanted, and would not be prevented from leaving. Then he went directly to the lottery office and claimed the prize. They wrote him a check on the spot. After taxes, he cleared about thirty million."

I leaned back in my chair and shook my head. "Wait a minute. You're buying this? Why would someone take a million dollars for a ticket that's worth thirty times that amount? Didn't Simon ask that question? He had to know it wasn't on the up-and-up."

"He claims he did ask when he replied to the e-mail. The guy said he was going through a messy divorce and was sure his evil, soon-to-be ex-wife would sue him for at least half, if not all of the winnings. Rather than let her have any, he'd sacrifice the big payoff for a measly one million."

"Okay, but why the James Bond exchange? Wasn't Simon suspicious at all about why the guy didn't want to be seen?"

"The guy was paranoid. He had a feeling his wicked wife had a suspicion about the ticket. He didn't want any trail that could lead back to him."

"And you believe this story?"

Sam let out an exasperated sigh. "I believe that Simon believes it. Let me rephrase that. I believe that Simon *wants* to believe it. Thirty million dollars could finance a lot of home construction, or a comfortable retirement."

"But, hasn't some law been broken here? Conspiracy? Anything?" I insisted.

"Not by Simon."

"Wait a minute. What about that woman who had a winning ticket and filed for divorce before she cashed it in so she wouldn't have to share it with her husband. Didn't he sue and the courts awarded the whole thing to him?"

"That's true, but Simon wasn't the one concealing assets."

"But he thought he was helping someone else conceal assets. Isn't that like being an accomplice to a crime?" I insisted.

Sam rubbed his tired eyes then ran his fingers through his hair. "You want me to go after Simon when we know he's not the murderer? Why waste our resources on him?"

"So, the killer has a million bucks, Simon has thirty-million, and Lou Winnomore's murder goes down in the annals of unsolved mysteries."

"Not necessarily. Simon did us one big favor in this whole mess. He recorded the serial numbers of the bills before he handed them over."

I raised my eyebrows. "Really? Why'd he do that if he thought everything was kosher?"

Sam smirked at me. "Because Simon is smart. He wanted a little insurance that if it wasn't above-board, he wouldn't be stuck holding the smoking gun."

"So this is your plan? Wait till the bills show up in circulation and nab the culprit?"

"It's worked in the past," Sam replied.

I rolled my eyes. "You know how many ways there are to launder money? The guy's already on to the fact that we know Lou was murdered. This whole Arthur Simon scenario proves that. You think he's going to stick around town and buy his groceries with that money? I bet he's already in Mexico. He'll put that money in a Mexican bank and the trail will hit a block wall right at the border."

Sam scowled at me. "You got any bright ideas?"

"You try checking out the source of the anonymous e-mail?" I asked.

"I got guys working on it right now. They don't sound hopeful."

"How about fingerprints on the locker and under the seat where they hid the key?"

"It would only take about a year to sort out the eighty-some-odd prints we'd probably find, half of which would not be complete enough to make any identification, and run them against our database. Then, if the guy was stupid enough to not wear gloves or wipe off his prints, and if he's already got a record, we might be lucky enough to get him."

"Do you ever see the glass half-full?" I asked.

"Only when it's whiskey."

I stood and headed for the door. I stopped with my hand on the knob. "You go ahead and wait for one of those bills to show up. I've got work to do."

Sam pounded his fist on his desk. "Not on this case, you don't!"

I ignored his comment as I walked out the door.

"I mean it! I'm not gonna lift a finger to save your scrawny little neck when you find it in a vice!" he hollered at me through the closed door.

"Oh, yes you will," I whispered to myself as I pushed my way out the door to the parking lot. "And you'll thank me when you get promoted for solving this murder."

Chapter Eight

I decided my best bet was to start with Chuck, the brother-in-law. He would probably know more about Lou Winno-more's family than anyone. I called ahead to let him know I'd be stopping by, but I didn't tell him why. He seemed like a very accommodating man on the phone, giving me block-by-block directions to his house. When I arrived, he was waiting at the front door to greet me. He was a plump, baldheaded man with a white mustache. He wore a plaid shirt and fire-engine-red suspenders, which held up a pair of brand new blue jeans. A pair of reading glasses sat perched on the end of his nose, and he had a newspaper rolled up and tucked under his arm.

"Hello. You must be Devonie," he called as I got out of my car.

"Yes. And you're Chuck?"

"That's me. Come on in. The wife is baking cookies. Oatmeal, I think."

I smiled and followed him into his kitchen. "Betty, this

is Devonie. She's the little gal who bought Lou's place," Chuck said to his wife, who was busy measuring out a cup of raisins into a bowl of oatmeal cookie dough. She was twice as plump as her husband.

"Nice to meet you," she replied. "Sorry I can't shake your hand, but I'm all gooey with dough," she continued, waving her pudgy, dough-covered fingers over the bowl to prove her point.

"Oh, don't worry. I know never to bother a chef when she's busy creating a masterpiece," I said, admiring a rack of cooling cookies. The aroma of cinnamon wafted to my nose. "They smell great."

Betty smiled proudly. "Help yourself. They're still warm from the oven."

Chuck grabbed two off the cooling rack and took a bite out of one. He pointed toward the rest. "Better hurry before I eat 'em all."

I took one and tasted it. It was wonderful—warm and chewy with lots of raisins and walnuts. It was clear to me why Chuck and Betty were a bit on the plump side, especially if she cooked like this routinely. "Mmm. Delicious."

Chuck handed me a napkin and pulled a chair out for me to sit at the table. "What can I do for you?" he asked.

"Thank you," I said, taking the seat. "I don't really know how to break this to you gently, so I guess I'll just tell you straight out."

Chuck frowned. "You mean about Lou?"

I was a little surprised. "What about Lou?" I asked.

"That someone killed him," Chuck said.

"You know?"

"Yes. A detective came by last night to talk to us. He told me what happened."

"Detective Wright?" I asked.

"That's him. Nice fellow. I told him all I could about Lou. Don't think I was much help."

I was more than a little irritated that Sam didn't tell me he'd spoken with Chuck. He told me the whole story about Arthur Simon, so why not Chuck? Maybe Chuck was right. Maybe he didn't have anything to offer to the investigation, so Sam didn't bring it up. I decided to give him the benefit of the doubt.

"So, did he ask you about the painting?" I asked.

"Painting? Oh, yes. The purple one. He wanted to know if I knew who painted it."

"Do you?" I asked.

"No. That picture just showed up on Lou's wall one day. I made a passing comment about it the day he hung it up. Think I might have made Lou mad."

"What did you say?" I asked.

"I think I said something like, 'Good thing Maggie's not around to see it.' She hated purple, you know."

"That's true," Betty said, as she dropped spoonfuls of cookie dough onto a baking sheet. "We were twins. She hated purple from the day we were born. Wouldn't wear it if her life depended on it. I always liked the color, so I wore it all the time. Worked out good because she'd hardly ever wanted to borrow my clothes."

"So he got the painting after she died?" I asked.

"Oh, yeah. I think he only had it a couple months before he died. Maggie'd been gone for a year or more," Chuck explained.

"You don't know where he got it, do you?"

Chuck shook his head. "No. After I said that Maggie wouldn't like it, he didn't want to talk about it anymore."

I tapped my fingers on the table. "Did you know he played the lottery?"

"Twice a week. Never missed a draw, except when Maggie died. You could wallpaper his house with that box full of all those tickets he bought. He quit for a while, but we told him he needed to get back into the routine of things. He got really down."

I nodded. I could certainly understand that. "Did you know the numbers he played?"

"You mean, like regular numbers?"

"Yes. Birthdays, anniversaries," I said.

"I didn't know he played any particular numbers."

I studied Chuck's face. My brain told me he could be lying, but something else said he was telling the truth. "What about his children? I understand he has a son and daughter?"

"Two sons, but Joey died right after Lou. Real sad," Chuck said. I detected a faint quiver in his voice.

"What about the other son?" I asked.

"Frankie? He's up in Norwalk. He, uh, he doesn't ever get out to visit anymore."

I knew there was a state mental hospital in Norwalk. I laced my fingers together, trying to come up with a tactful way to ask if Frankie was still crazy. "Metropolitan State Hospital?"

Chuck nodded. "Yeah. As long as he takes his medication, he's okay, but when he doesn't, boy look out."

"What's the matter with him?" I asked.

"Paranoid schizophrenia. Put a scare into Lou and Maggie about fifteen or twenty years ago. Secret Service came knocking on their door one day wanting to know if Frankie was their son. Seems he'd made some threats against the president, and they were taking them seriously."

"Was he serious?" I asked.

"He's sick. The old Frankie was a sweet kid, but that disease, it takes over the brain. Got to where he didn't know what was real and what was imagined. He thought the president was the devil. I think if he had the chance, he'd have done what he said. They had him committed and he never came home again."

"There was that one time he escaped," Betty reminded him.

"Oh, yeah. About five years ago, he went AWOL and hitchhiked all the way home. Lou and Maggie tried to keep him with them and take care of him, but he'd stopped taking his medication. They just couldn't handle him. They finally called the hospital and asked them to come get him."

"That's too bad," I said. "Maybe someday we'll be able to cure that disease. What about Lou's daughter? I heard she's in Africa?"

"Sister Nellie. That child wanted to help anyone and anything she could from the time she could walk. Always bringing home animals that were hurt or hungry. Lou's place looked like a regular zoo while she was growing up. Lou thought she'd become a veterinarian, but when she got to be a teenager, she quit bringing home animals and started bringing home people instead. Homeless she'd find wandering the streets. Drunks she found passed out in the gutters. Troubled runaways who couldn't go home. Lou finally had to put his foot down. He could handle the pets, but that's where he drew the line."

"Was she angry?" I asked.

"Angry? That girl would like to have boiled her father in oil when he made her turn those people out. She thought Maggie would be on her side, but when Maggie backed up Lou, Nellie felt deserted. She did her time there at home until she graduated from high school, then she joined the Peace Corps and took off for all those third-world countries."

"She never came home?" I asked.

"Oh, she comes home every few years for a short visit, mostly for appearances, but we haven't seen her for six years. When she heard that Lou and Maggie sent Frankie back to the hospital, she disowned the entire family."

Betty gently slid a tray of cookies into the oven. "I'd like to see her try to handle that brother of hers. She had no idea what he was like," she said, closing the oven door and setting the timer.

I started thinking about poor Lou Winnomore. It seemed his life was riddled with difficulties. "What about his other son? The one who passed away?"

"Joey. There's another sad story. I'm just glad Lou wasn't around for that. It would have torn him apart," Chuck said.

"What happened?"

"Joey committed suicide, must have been about two weeks after Lou died. That's when we found out about the mess he'd gotten himself into. Shot himself in the head with his service revolver. Bridgett would have killed him herself if he hadn't done the job first."

"Bridgett? That's his wife?"

Chuck nodded. "He'd had an affair and the other woman turned up pregnant. Boy, everything hit the fan when that news came out."

"Does Bridgett live around here?" I asked.

"Oh, yeah. Over near the university. She's trying to get a degree in something, I don't remember what, so she can get a better job, now that she's a single parent.

"You don't know what she's studying?"

"No. She's pretty much divorced herself from Joey's family. It's like she thinks we supported what he did."

I wondered what Bridgett might be capable of. The old saying about a woman scorned crossed my mind. She could have killed her cheating husband, then killed her father-in-law and stolen the lottery ticket to avoid splitting her son's inheritance with the other boy. "Her name's Bridgett Winnomore?"

"As far as I know, she hasn't changed her name. If it weren't for the boy, she'd probably go back to her maiden name."

I took the last bite of my cookie and wiped my fingers on the napkin. "What about the other woman? Is she still in the picture?"

Betty laughed. "Oh, she's in the picture, alright. Never saw a greedier woman in my entire life. I bet she spends more time in her lawyer's office finding ways to get her hooks in other people's money than she does at home with that baby. You know the ordeal we went through to sell the house because of her."

"Do you think I could have her address? And Bridgett's too?"

"Sure. That detective already has their addresses. You might run into him if you go to see them," Chuck said as he reached for a pen and paper and an address book near his phone."

I certainly hope I don't run into Sam. He'd kill me if he thought I was interfering with his investigation. I thanked Chuck for the information, and Betty for the cookies. She wrapped up a half-dozen for me to take.

I stared at the paper with the women's addresses and wondered whom to visit first. I struggled with the decision for a while, then decided that under the circumstances, I'd rather face a bunch of mental hospital workers than either of those two women.

It's quite a long drive from San Diego to Norwalk, so I stopped for lunch along the way. I'd just been seated in a booth near a window when Sam surprised me by sliding into the seat opposite me.

"Sam? What are you doing here?"

He opened a menu and studied the lunch specials. "Following you," he said, still reading the menu.

"Why?"

"You're headed for Norwalk."

"So?"

He closed the menu and pushed it aside. "What do you think you're going to do once you get there?"

"Find out if Frankie was AWOL when Lou died. Maybe see if he does any painting," I replied, indignantly.

Sam laughed. "No one there is going to tell you anything. You're just some stranger off the street."

"I considered that. I had a plan," I defended.

"Okay, I'll bite. What's your plan?"

I opened my menu and began reading. "How'd you find me, anyway?"

"It was easy. I figured you'd go see Chuck, so I waited till you showed up, then tailed you here. You really ought to learn the tricks of the trade if you're going to be a private investigator."

"Who said I want to be a private investigator?"

"Walks like a duck, quacks like a duck . . ."

"Talks like a duck," I corrected.

"Must be a duck. Why don't you apply for your license? I could cut you a little more slack if you were legit."

I continued reading the menu.

"So, come on. What's your plan?" he insisted.

I scowled at him over the menu.

"Look. I've already talked to the folks at Metropolitan. Frank hasn't been off the grounds for years," Sam informed me.

"You talked to him?" I asked.

"No. I talked to one of the doctors. Frank's not our guy."

I closed my menu. "You owe me lunch."

"I was hoping you'd forget."

"Fat chance."

"Okay. I'll buy lunch, then we head back to San Diego."

"No way. That wasn't the deal. You owe me lunch. I've come this far, and I'm not going back until I see Frankie," I insisted.

Sam followed me to the hospital, but I asked him to wait outside until I was finished. I walked into the reception area and glanced around. I could see a recreation room at the end of a hallway with people sitting randomly at various tables. A group of patients stared at a television that played an old "I Love Lucy" rerun. Trying to look like I'd been there before, I began strolling toward the room. A woman sitting behind a desk caught me before I could wander any further.

"Can I help you?" she asked.

"Yes. Hi. I'm looking for Frank Winnomore. I understand he's a patient here?"

She scrutinized me over her glasses. "Are you on the visitor list?"

I shook my head. "I wanted to know if he wants any of the things from his late father's home before I sell them."

The woman smiled. "That's very considerate of you, but we have strict rules. Only approved visitors can see the patients. If you're not on the list, then I'm afraid—"

"Nellie? Is that you?" a voice called from the TV room down the hall. A tall, thin man with long black hair trotted toward me, squinting as he bounced. He hadn't shaved for a week, and I wasn't sure he'd bathed, either. My lungs didn't want to take a breath as soon as he got within arms length. "It is you! You came to see me, after all these years!" he called, stretching his arms out to embrace me.

"Frank? This is Nellie?" the woman behind the desk asked.

Frank? Could this be the Frank I'm looking for? I played along and put my arms around him. "Frank. It's been a long time," I said, patting his back and holding my breath.

Frank released me from his embrace and clutched my shoulders. "This is my dear sister, Nellie," he said to the woman behind the counter. "I knew she'd come back one day, and here she is. Give her a visitor badge, Lucy. I want to take her on a tour."

Lucy eyed me suspiciously. By the looks of her, she could have been a prison guard assigned to keep Charles Manson in line. She had the closest thing to a flattop haircut I'd ever seen on a woman. I halfway expected her to step out from behind the desk and frisk me. "Do you have any identification?" she asked.

I gave her a helpless look.

"She's a missionary from Africa, Lucy! You think she runs around with a driver's license and a charge card? Come on. She's my sister. I haven't had a visitor all year. Give her a badge and let me show her around," Frank insisted.

"Passport?" Lucy suggested.

I shook my head. "Back at the hotel."

"Lu-ceee," Frank whined, holding his hands in a pleading fashion.

Lucy caved in and handed me a pen to sign in, and a badge to wear on my shirt pocket. She also shot me a look that could kill if it were loaded.

Frank grabbed me by the hand and led me toward a glass door that led outside. Suddenly, we were in a large park-like setting surrounded on all sides by the hospital walls. It was an atrium filled with plants and flowers and picnic tables. There was one other patient sitting at a table, playing with a puzzle. Frank bumped his chair and told him to scram. He collected his toys and scurried for the door. Then Frank took the man's chair and sat down. I took the seat opposite him.

"So, who are you?" he asked.

"I'm not Nellie?" I replied.

He laughed. "Nellie is six-foot-two and has hair on her arms like a gorilla."

A vision of Nellie flashed through my mind. "Oh. Well then, why did you say—"

"I'm not in here for my hearing. I heard you tell Lucy about Dad's stuff. You bought his place?" he asked.

I nodded. "Yes."

"They'd never let you see me unless you were on their precious list. Nellie's the only one on the list who Lucy hasn't seen before."

I stared at this man wearing hospital garb and wondered what I should think about him. Aside from speaking very slowly and moving somewhat sluggishly, he seemed quite aware. It didn't take long to deduce that Frankie was sharper than anyone gave him credit for. He noticed my stare.

"What? You were expecting a moron? I'm schizoid, not retarded," he snapped.

I smiled apologetically. "I'm sorry. I don't know what I expected. You seem very—"

"Shut up, Melvin!" Frank hissed at the empty chair next to him. He shook his finger angrily at the vacant seat. "Mind your manners, or I'll make you leave."

I watched Frank reprimand some imaginary person sitting next to him, and wondered if he really saw someone there, or if he was play-acting. He kept shooting quick, sideways glances at me while he scolded Melvin. I caught him suppressing a grin.

He finally relaxed and turned his attention back to me. "You have to excuse Melvin for his crudeness. He thinks you're quite pretty, but he has no class. He won't say another word, I promise."

I smiled and nodded, as if I understood, but I couldn't really relate to Frank's disorder. I never had imaginary friends as a child. I never conversed with beings that weren't really there. I cleared my throat uneasily and glanced at the empty chair. "Do you really see someone in that chair?" I asked.

Frank's smile faded. "You don't?"

"No."

There was a long, uncomfortable silence, then he burst out into boisterous laughter. "I guess that's why I'm in here and you're not."

I joined him in his laughter for a moment, then I stopped. "I think you're jerking my chain, Frank. I think you get a kick out of getting reactions out of people."

Frank's face turned serious. He laced his fingers together and put them on the table. "What do you have of my dad's stuff?"

I relaxed. It occurred to me that Frank might be just a little bit dangerous and I probably should not have confronted him that way. I was glad that his behavior turned rational rather than radical.

"Everything, but I don't imagine you can keep it all here. I found a few photo albums I thought you might want."

His face lit up. "Pictures?"

"Uh huh. I brought them with me. They're in my car."

"That'd be great. How about my little league trophies?"

I frowned. "I didn't bring those. They'd been broken," I said.

"Broken? How?"

"Kids broke into your father's house after he died. They vandalized the place."

"Creeps. Did they catch them?" he asked.

"I think so. Did you know about a painting your father bought after your mother died? He had it hanging in the living room."

"My dad never bought a painting in his life."

"Are you sure? I mean, you haven't lived at home for a long time."

"He came to visit me every week until he died. Spent the whole day with me. He hated long stretches without talking, so he made lists of every little thing he did that week so we'd have stuff to talk about. He would have told me if he did something like spend money on a painting."

I was disappointed, but at least my trip wasn't for nothing. Frank would get the family photo albums, and I was glad for that. "Well, I'll get those albums for you," I said, as I stood to leave.

"But I do remember him telling me someone *gave* him a painting."

I sat back down. "You do?"

"Yeah. He said he felt a little guilty for hanging it up, because he liked it even though it was purple, and my mom hated purple."

I perked up. "That's the one. Who gave it to him?"

"Heck if I know. A friend of his, I think. Maybe someone who lived in the neighborhood. All I remember is he said he carried it home on foot, and it was sort of big and awkward."

I felt a sudden urge to dangle this new evidence in front of Sam's arrogant face. He thinks he's so smart.

"Thanks, Frank. I'll get those albums for you now."

Chapter Nine

I balanced a peach pie in my left hand as I rang Bob's and Agnes' doorbell with my right. That triggered a reaction in Tiger, their cocker spaniel, who I could hear frantically barking on the other side of the door. Agnes opened the door, hanging on to his collar. She gawked at me for a moment.

"Hi, Agnes. It's me, Devonie, from next door. Remember? You brought my husband and I flowers from your garden?"

After a few seconds, the old wheel cogs clicked and she remembered. "Oh, yes." Then her gaze shot past me, searching for something beyond her front porch. "Did you bring your husband?" she asked, straining to see around the corner of the house. Tiger struggled to free himself from her grip. She picked him up in her arms.

"Not today, I'm afraid. He's working. I wanted to bring you and Bob this pie, though. Sort of a thank you for calling us the other night to warn us about the intruder."

"Who is it, pumpkin?" Bob's voice called, trailing from some room at the back of the house. A moment later, he was at Agnes' side, with his arm around her shoulders.

"It's that girl from next door, you know, the doctor's wife," Agnes replied.

I smiled. "Devonie," I reminded her. "I brought you a pie. It's peach."

Bob's face lit up like a Malibu brushfire. "Who told you I love peach pie? Come on in," he said, pushing the screen door open to allow me through.

Agnes handed Tiger off to Bob, I assume to protect me from having my leg taken off. She snatched the pie from my hands and scurried off to the kitchen with it. Bob led me from the foyer to the living room, where he released Tiger into the backyard. I noticed the floor plan of their house was nearly identical to Rancho Costa Little, only in reverse.

Unlike Lou, Bob and Agnes had kept their home up-to-date. Ceramic tile floors in the entry and kitchen, and polished granite countertops made the home look much more contemporary than it really was. They had installed skylights in the kitchen, which brightened it up considerably. Rather than carpet, the remainder of the house boasted hardwood floors, which were finished in a tone a little darker than I liked, but it was very pretty. The place was gorgeous.

I gazed around the living room. "Your house is beautiful," I said. "Would you mind giving me a tour?"

Bob's chest puffed up like a rooster. "Did all the work myself," he bragged. "Come on. Wait till you see what I did with the bathrooms."

I followed Bob through the house, admiring every detail. I discreetly examined each painting on every wall, checking for signatures. When we returned to the living room, I paid particular attention to a painting hanging over their sofa.

"This is great," I said. The painting depicted a view of the ocean on a sunny day from a white-railed porch. Vibrant flowers planted in clay pots scattered around the deck added color and charm. A child's plastic pail and shovel sat in the sand a short distance from the steps, adding interest to the piece. If you looked at it long enough, you could almost hear the waves gently rolling in.

"Like it?" Bob replied, straightening the frame a tinge.

"I love it," I said, searching the lower corners for a signature. "Where'd you get it?"

Bob puffed up again, and I wondered if he was going to confess to be the artist. "Best art deal I've ever made," he said. "Bought it down at a little art show they have in the park every year. The artist was an unknown at the time. I finagled the price down to half of what he was asking. Now, he's a hotshot with a deal for calendars and greeting cards. His work is worth thousands, and I have an original."

I admired the painting a moment longer. "You know, I used to dabble in art when I was younger. I had a little talent, but not enough motivation to ever pursue it seriously."

Bob motioned for me to take a seat on the sofa. He sat down in a leather recliner across from me. He looked like a king sitting on his throne. "That talent's a gift. You're lucky to have it." He leaned forward and straightened the coffee table books sitting in front of him. "When you don't use a gift like that, it's like giving a child a toy she won't play with. You watch with anticipation, waiting for the little one to play, and when she doesn't, you're disappointed. Me? I couldn't draw a straight line with a ruler. My only gift is knowing good art when I see it. Now Agnes, she's a different story."

I perked up. "Really?"

"Yes. You should see her needlepoint. Magnificent. She did a life-size of John Wayne that'll knock your socks off."

"Life-size? That must have taken years," I said.

Agnes entered the room carrying a tray with three slices of pie and a pitcher of ice tea. Bob helped her with the tray. "How long did John Wayne take you?" he asked.

"Three years," she proudly replied.

"Gave it to my grandson for his birthday. He uses it for a bedspread," Bob continued.

"I'd like to see it sometime. Do you paint, also?" I asked her.

Agnes handed me a slice of pie and a fork. "No. Just the needlework, and I knit and crochet. Arthritis is making it hard to do that much. Now, I spend most of my time in the garden."

"I was just wondering," I continued. "Do you know the painting Lou had hanging in his living room?"

Bob and Agnes exchanged glances. "The purple mountains?" Bob replied.

"That's the one. Do you know where he got it?" I asked.

Bob scratched his head and looked at Agnes. "Gee, pumpkin, you recall where Lou got that?"

Agnes shook her head. "I never really cared for it. Too much of the same color. I like more variety."

"I was told that someone in the neighborhood may have

given it to him. Are there any artists living around here that you know of?" I asked.

"There's Wally, but that painting's not his style. He does what they call impressionist art. Looks like something my three-year-old granddaughter could do, but the critics love it."

"Besides, Wally would never give a painting away," Agnes added. "Wouldn't even donate one for our annual church auction."

I glanced out the window and noticed Tiger playing with a red-and-white ball in the backyard. He tossed it in the air and tried to catch it. "What's that your dog has?" I asked, pointing to the unusual ball.

Bob squinted to see what I was pointing at. "Oh, that's his float."

"Float?" I asked.

"Yeah. You know. For fishing," Bob explained. "I think it was one of Lou's. It showed up in our backyard right after he passed away."

"It did? How do you suppose it got in your yard?"

"Well, Lou just got back from a fishing trip with his son that night. I figured he never had a chance to put his gear away before he died. That's about the time those kids were breaking into houses around here."

"Rotten kids," Agnes had to throw into the conversation.

Bob nodded in agreement. "Anyhow, Tiger was probably barking up a storm over in our yard, so they may have tossed him anything that looked like a ball to shut him up. He loves balls, as you can see."

I watched Tiger throw the ball and run after it till his

tongue hung nearly to the ground. "Does he ever get tired?" I asked.

"Oh, yeah. Pretty soon he'll quit and go lay down," Bob replied.

"So Lou had gone on a fishing trip just before he died?" I asked.

"Yeah. Him and Joey went up to Big Bear that weekend. We watched the place for him."

"He was gone for two days?"

"That's right. He left early Saturday morning and didn't get home until late Sunday night. Joey found him the next morning. He came by to drop off the fish they'd caught after he cleaned them."

I thought about this for a moment. "How did Joey get in the house?"

"I don't know. Maybe he knew about Lou's hide-a-key over the door. He grew up in that house. Wouldn't surprise me if he had his own key," Bob said.

Bob noticed my troubled expression. "You're not still worried about someone having keys to the place, are you?"

I shook my head. "No. I had the locks changed. I'm sure no one is interested in getting into the house anymore."

"I almost forgot. Did they ever catch the guy who was in there the other night when I called you?"

"No. He disappeared before the police got there. Did you ever see anything other than lights inside the house that night?"

Bob thought for a moment, then shook his head. "Never saw a car or anything, if that's what you're after. And I kept my eye on the place from the second I called you right up until the police car showed up. Whoever was in there snuck out like a cat in the dark."

Agnes cleared her throat. "Not to change the subject, but why the sudden interest in that painting?" she asked.

I studied Bob's face, then Agnes'. They didn't strike me as murderers, but I wasn't ready to cross them off of my suspect list, just yet. "Oh, I just wanted to know where I could get another one to go with it."

Just as Bob had predicted, Tiger got tired of his game with the fishing float and found a shady spot under a tree to rest. I set my empty pie plate on the tray and stood up, indicating that I was ready to leave. Bob thanked me for the pie, and Agnes insisted that I bring Craig with me the next time I came to visit. I promised I would.

I was developing a clearer picture of what may have happened to Lou. The murderer must have known that Lou would be gone for the weekend. If the murderer knew Lou well enough to know his personal lottery numbers, he probably also knew of Lou's fishing trip. The killer probably discovered the winning numbers on Saturday night, and recognized them as Lou's. He would have had only about twenty-four hours to come up with, and execute his plan. I wondered how someone could get his hands on cyanide on such short notice. I drove to the police lab to talk to Eric.

I interrupted Eric in the middle of his tuna fish sandwich. He gladly offered me a chair at his small desk, and half of his lunch. "You talk to Sam lately?" he asked.

"Not today. I thought I'd go see him after I talk to you."

"What's up?" he asked, still chewing a mouthful of food.

"I was wondering how someone could get their hands on cyanide? It can't be that easy, can it?"

Eric quickly nodded his head and swallowed a bite of his sandwich. "Cyanide's used commercially in metal recovery, like extracting gold or silver from their ores. It's also used in electroplating metals like gold, silver, copper and platinum."

Eric opened a bag of potato chips and offered them to me. I removed one from the bag and ate it.

"Now you know you can't eat just one," he said, shoving the bag toward me. I smiled and took a handful. I couldn't remember the last time I'd eaten a potato chip.

"So, if you worked for a mining company—"

"Or a jewelry or metal-plating company. Some chemical supply firms sell it. You can get the stuff. It's not like we're talking about plutonium."

"And it's a powder?" I asked.

Eric nodded. "Or it can be in the form of a pellet. You heard about the mining company helicopter that accidentally dropped a couple tons of it in some jungle somewhere? Those were pellets. What a mess that was."

"So it was probably pellets that our murderer used. That's why he had to grind them up and got the paint pigment mixed up with the cyanide," I suggested.

Eric nodded in agreement as he gulped down milk from a thermos that left a white mustache on his upper lip.

I thanked Eric for the information and the chips, and headed for Sam's office.

When I walked in, Sam was busy hanging a white board on his wall.

"What's that for?" I asked.

"It's supposed to help solve crimes," he replied, still working the screwdriver.

"How?"

He set his tools down and stepped back to admire his work. "By making the scenes more visible. Kind of like a storyboard. Sometimes it helps to see all your clues at once. We have one in the bullpen. I thought I'd like to have one in here too. See if it helps."

I nodded. "Sort of like a big version of your little notebook," I offered.

"Sort of, except I can't carry this around with me."

I stared at the board for a moment. "It's crooked," I said.

"What?"

"Look. It's not level. That side is higher than this side."

Sam backed up a couple feet and stared at the board. "It looks straight to me," he argued.

"Did you use a level?"

"No. I measured from the ceiling."

"How do you know the ceiling is level?" I asked.

Sam dropped the screwdriver into his desk drawer and shoved it closed. "Is there a reason for this visit, or did you just drop by to bug me?"

"I came by to talk about Lou Winnomore. I was just over talking to Eric in the lab."

Sam was busy removing assorted colors of dry-erase pens from a box. He placed them one-by-one on the tray at the bottom of the white-board. He turned the box over and shook it until the eraser fell out. "So talk."

I stood up and walked over to the board. I picked up the blue pen and removed the cap.

Sam looked at me as if I'd just taken his wallet. "What are you doing?" he demanded.

"I'm going to use your new tool to help solve this crime. You mind?"

Sam snatched the pen from my hand. "You can't be the first one to write on my board. I'll do the writing."

I returned to my seat. "Fine, but don't forget to keep the pen covered when you're not using it, or it'll dry out."

"I know that," he scoffed. "I was going to do this anyway, so don't go thinking this is your idea."

"Okay. Okay. What do you think about starting with a timeline?" I suggested.

Sam smiled and pointed the pen at me. "Good idea." He drew a horizontal line on the board and made a couple of small vertical marks on it. "Let's start with the purchase of the ticket."

"Good. That had to happen some time between Wednesday night and early Saturday morning," I said.

"No. He could have bought the ticket right up until the time of the draw on Saturday night," Sam replied.

"I don't think so. Lou left early on Saturday morning to go on a fishing trip with his son. He would have already bought the ticket for Saturday night's game."

"How do you know that?" he asked.

"I talked to the neighbors this morning. They told me." Sam glared at me.

I pointed toward his hand. "Your pen is going to dry out."

"What else did they tell you?"

"I'll get to that. Just write down what I said."

He scribbled something small and illegible. "I can't read

that. You've got a whole big board there. You can write a little bigger, can't you?"

He snapped the cap back on the pen and marched across the room to where I sat. "Here," he said, slapping the pen in my hand. "I'm going to save myself a lot of grief and just let you do it."

I filled out the timeline with everything we'd learned so far. Then, I began a list at one end of the board. "This is everything we know about the killer. He was probably a friend of Lou's. He knew Lou's regular numbers. He knew about the fishing trip. He had easy access to cyanide. He either knew about the hidden key, or he had a key to Lou's house."

"Or, he picked the lock," Sam offered.

"Maybe. Okay. What else? He's an artist and he mixes his own paints. He lives in the neighborhood. He's computer savvy. He has a million dollars in cash stashed away somewhere. He—"

Sam's phone rang and interrupted my train of thought. He listened intently to whomever called, scribbling furiously in his notebook. "Thanks, Dan. I'll be right down," he said, then hung up the phone.

He leaned back in his chair and laced his fingers behind his head. With all the smugness he could muster, he said, "And he just spent one of those serial-numbered bills right here in sunny Southern California. Write that down, Sherlock."

Chapter Ten

As it turned out, the hundred-dollar bill was part of the daily cash receipts for Disneyland. Sam told me over the phone shortly after I'd met with him. It was my turn to be smug.

"So, that narrows your potential suspects down to, what, fifty-thousand?" I said.

"Go ahead and gloat. This is good. This means our guy isn't being too careful. He'll screw up sooner or later, and we'll grab him."

"Yeah. Maybe next time, he'll drop one of those bills at Sea World or, hey, maybe he'll head over to Vegas," I replied sarcastically.

Sam hung up on me. I'd pushed him a little too far. That was okay. I started thinking that the Disneyland clue might actually be useful. Both Bridgett Winnomore and Raven Covina had kids. Granted, Raven's was a small baby, but people take babies to Disneyland all the time. I was never told how old Bridgett's son was, but kids of any age love to go to Disneyland.

I dug through my purse and pulled out Raven Covina's address. I had no idea what story I'd use to convince her to talk to me, but I figured I'd come up with something on the way to her house.

She actually lived in an apartment—one of the older complexes in the area. I pulled into one of the visitor parking spots and gazed around the area. My eyes stopped on an old Volkswagen bus, parked in one of the tenants' spots. It was painted psychedelic. I almost expected to see a Deadhead roll out of the van. I noticed a beach scene painted in the lower rear corner. The painting was very good. There was some writing on the seascape that was too small for me to read. I got out of my car and approached the van. I squinted. I could see brushstrokes in the paint, which seemed out of place on a vehicle.

"Bahama's Mama?" I read. The meaning nearly escaped me until I remembered that Raven Covina had named her son Bahama Breeze. I stared at the bus. My eyes moved over the painting. Could this artist be the same one who painted the purple mountains? Could Raven Covina be the artist? Could she be the murderer? I scratched my head and wandered all around the bus, studying the artwork. I had some problems with keeping Raven as a suspect. She didn't live within walking distance of Lou's house, so it's not likely that he carried the painting all the way home from here. The question that nagged at me most was why Raven would give Lou anything? I would not imagine they were close. I even doubted they knew each other. What kind of man introduces his mistress to his father?

I stood there, gawking at the van, when a woman approached me. She had an infant in a sling-like garment hung around her neck and over one shoulder. "Ain't it somethin'?" she boasted, stretching an arm out and strutting along the side of the bus like Vanna White on "Wheel of Fortune." Under the baby sling, she wore a long, colorful robe-like dress. Her feet jingled with little copper bells attached to her sandals, which were brown leather and laced halfway up her calves. Her black hair was pulled back in a ponytail and separated into a collection of braids. Her skin was smooth and brown. She had a very exotic appearance and reminded me of some tarot-card-reading psychic I'd seen advertising on TV. I thought she might be from somewhere like Jamaica or Haiti. I'd probably find out later that she's from Burbank.

"Is this yours?" I asked, nodding toward the bus.

"Yeah. You like it?"

"It's . . . unique. Did you do the artwork?"

She smiled and cooed at the baby in her sling. "Most of it. Are you here to see somebody?"

"Huh? Oh. Yes, but she wasn't home. I was just leaving when I saw your artwork."

"It is eye-catching, ain't it?"

I nodded. "It sure is. Are you an artist by trade?"

She danced a small teddy bear in front of her baby's face and talked baby talk to him, smiling all the time. "I do pinstriping down at Shawn's Auto Body. All the guys in the shop call me an artist. Have you been over to University Bowling Alley?"

I shook my head.

"I painted the mural on the wall in the bar. It's a masterpiece. My finest work," she boasted.

"Really? A landscape?"

"No. Underwater seascape. Whales, dolphins, squid, jellyfish. If it lives underwater, it's in my mural."

"I love art. I'm somewhat of a collector," I told her.

Her eyes lit up. "I should show you my stuff . . . I mean, my work."

"I'd love to see it. My name's Devonie, by the way."

She cradled the baby with one hand and offered to shake my hand with her other. "I'm Raven. Good to meet you."

I had my confirmation. She's Raven Covina, and she's an artist. I would have moved her up a notch or two on my suspect list, but her style didn't look the same as the painting in Lou's house.

"Are you on your way somewhere, or do you have time to show me your other work?" I asked.

"I was just going to check my laundry. Me and the baby like to go outside for walks in the sunshine."

"Great. I can help you carry it back, then maybe I could see your paintings."

Raven smiled so wide her teeth looked like piano keys. I wondered if anyone besides the bowling alley bar people had ever shown an interest in her work.

"Come on," she said, leading the way to the apartment complex laundry room.

When we walked into the laundry room, a large woman in a pair of green sweat pants with a clashing orange T-shirt was pulling an armload of clothes out of a dryer. Raven stood in the middle of the room, looking all around.

"Where's my basket, Rowena?" she asked, more accusingly than neighborly.

Rowena hoisted her basket onto a table. "How should I know?"

" 'Cause I left it right there on that table, and now it's gone. You're the only one here. You see somebody take it?"

Rowena shook her head. "I didn't see nobody take your basket. You oughta know better than to leave it layin' around, girl. I never leave nothin' around this place. I don't even leave my clothes in the machines without stayin' and watchin'. Otherwise, they just up and disappear."

Raven got right up into Rowena's face. "So you been here the whole time? And you didn't see who took my basket?"

Rowena wasn't backing down. I hoped I wasn't going to see a fight break out, especially with that tiny baby in the middle of it. "I told you, I didn't see nothin'. Whoever took your basket must've done it before I got here."

Raven stomped over to a dryer and swung the door open. "Shoot! They took my clothes! All my baby's shirts and pajamas! Where are they, Rowena?"

Rowena calmly picked up her basket of clothes and headed for the door. "They ain't here. That's all I know. Next time, you better sit your little self in one of those chairs and watch your stuff, otherwise you won't have nothin' but that hippie dress you got on."

Raven slammed the dryer door closed and stuck her tongue out at Rowena's back as she walked out the door.

I leaned against one of the washers and waited for Raven

to cool down a little. "You should report it to the manager. Maybe they can help," I offered.

"Yeah, right. They won't do anything. Last month someone took my bike and they didn't lift a finger. Had it chained to the railing and someone just sawed the metal. They still haven't even fixed the railing."

I scratched my head. "Well, maybe you should do what Rowena said and watch your clothes from now on. It's better than losing them."

Raven headed for the door. "Guess I'll have to. I can't think of anything more boring than sitting and waiting for clothes to get washed and dried."

I followed her out of the laundry room and toward her apartment. "Do you like to read?" I asked her.

"Used to read those crazy romance novels. Had me thinking a prince might come rescue me someday. Gave them up when I realized they'd never come true," she replied over her shoulder.

I wasn't really surprised when I walked into Raven's apartment. She had a major jungle theme going on. The walls were papered with a jute-like covering and the trim was painted with zebra stripes. A wooden giraffe that nearly reached the ceiling stood in the corner of the living room. I wondered if Raven carved it herself. The wicker furniture matched a fan, turning slowly from the ceiling.

I followed her to the room she called her studio. On the way, I noticed a small cutout with hookups for a small, stacked washer and dryer. "Why don't you just get your own washer and dryer? You've got the space, and then you wouldn't have to worry about your stuff getting taken," I suggested.

"Can't afford it," she replied as she led the way into her studio, which was just a small, second bedroom.

Why couldn't she afford it? She'd just gotten one sixth of the proceeds from the sale of Rancho Costa Little. But then I remembered, it was for the baby. I bet the courts made her put it in a fund that couldn't be touched until he's eighteen.

I walked into the room and my eyes nearly fell out of my head. Her work was astounding. I was amazed at her versatility. She was equally as talented at portraits as she was at landscapes and still-lifes. "Wow," I said. "You're really good."

Raven smiled and touched one of the paintings to check its dryness. "Thank you," she said, graciously.

Some of the work was black and white, probably pen and ink. Some I could tell was done in pencil or charcoal. Most of the pieces were in color. "What's your medium?" I asked.

"I mostly work with oils," she said. The baby started to get fussy and she tried to bounce him back into happiness. It wasn't working. "I'll be right back," she said, as she disappeared out of the room.

I looked at paintings stacked against the wall, six deep. Every one was appealing in its own way. None of them were monotone landscapes, and they were all signed. As much as I wanted to believe I'd found the artist of the purple painting, and the lottery-ticket-stealing murderer, I just didn't think Raven was the culprit.

I could hear Raven singing an old Sonny and Cher song,

"I've Got You, Babe" to the baby in the other room. I continued looking through the paintings when one in particular caught my eye. It was a garden scene with happy, summer flowers like daisies and sunflowers. In the middle of the garden was an empty chair and next to it, a banjo propped against a shade tree. I pulled the painting out to the front of the stack and stood back to admire it.

Raven returned, this time without the baby. "I put him down for a nap," she said. "What do you think about that one?" she asked, nodding toward the banjo painting.

"I love it. It would go perfect in my house. What are you asking for it?"

Raven gaped at me as though I were asking her if she wanted her million dollars in tens or twenties. "Really? You want to buy it?"

"If the price is right," I answered.

From what Chuck's wife, Betty, told me, Raven was a greedy, self-serving gold digger with a talent for latching onto other people's money. This wasn't the impression I got, but she hadn't named her price, yet.

"I don't know. What do you think it's worth?" she said.

I stared at the paintings, there must have been a hundred stored in that little room. None of them were framed, or looked as though they'd been displayed anywhere.

"Don't you sell on a regular basis?" I asked.

Raven seemed a little embarrassed. "No. I never knew if they were good enough."

"What? They're terrific. You mean you don't display them anywhere?"

"Where would I?"

I was amazed. There must have been hundreds, maybe

even thousands of hours of work invested in these paintings, and they just sat in this little room.

"There are dozens of galleries near here. Why don't you pick out two or three of your favorites to show some of them?"

"You think they'd like them?"

How could anyone so talented be so insecure? She must never have received any encouragement or praise as a child. It seemed funny, because she was more than willing to boast about her bowling-alley mural and her decorated bus, but those weren't considered serious art. What I'd seen in her little studio could put her on the road to a promising career in the art world.

"I'd like to have this painting. I'll have a brand new washer and dryer delivered and set up for you. How does that sound?"

Raven's eyes welled up with tears. "Oh my God. You know how much those cost?"

"You need them and I don't want to see your poor baby's clothes stolen anymore. And I want you to get these paintings in a gallery. You're way too talented to keep them locked away where no one can enjoy them."

I called Jason at his appliance shop and asked him to deliver the new washer and dryer as soon as he could. I knew he had several in stock, and I promised to buy him lunch if he could deliver them within the hour. He balked, as usual, but I have a way of getting on his nerves to the point where he'll do anything to get me to leave him alone.

While we waited for Jason, Raven offered me some sort of mango-strawberry tea. I sat in her wicker rocking chair and gazed around at the safari décor.

"Do you ever mix your own paints? You know, with dry pigment?" I asked as Raven poured the iced tea.

"Oh, no. That's for the real picky artists. I had a teacher who made us do it for one of his classes, but it seemed like a lot of work when I could just buy them already mixed."

"You took art classes?"

"At the university. I was an art major, but I had to drop out. Money, you know."

"When were you in school?"

"I quit a couple years ago."

I recalled that Lou's ex-daughter-in-law was attending the university.

"What was the teacher's name—the one who made you mix your own paint?" I asked.

Raven thought for a moment. "Champion. He was a good teacher." She grinned like a schoolgirl. "And boy was he cute."

Jason finally arrived with the washer and dryer and hooked them up. I wrote him a check and asked him to wait for me by his truck.

Raven wrapped my new painting in heavy brown paper and handed it to me. "Thank you so much," she said, with sincere gratitude.

"Thank you. And I want to see your paintings in a gallery soon. I'll be asking around for your work, so don't disappoint me."

Jason saw me coming with the painting and helped me get it in my car. "What was that all about?" he asked.

"I'll tell you over lunch."

"We'll have to do lunch next week. I have more deliveries to make," he said.

"Okay. Just let me know when."

I didn't expect to like Raven Covina before I met her. After all, she was a self-serving, greedy, home-wrecker, and I wouldn't normally have any use for someone like that. Maybe as I've gotten older, I've become more tolerant, or maybe Raven just needed a lucky break in life. It's possible she didn't know Joey Winnomore was married when she got involved with him. Men have been known to lie about such things.

Since I had the afternoon free, I drove over to the mall and bought a basketful of baby clothes for Raven's baby. I had the store box it up and sent it to her address.

She wasn't on my suspect list anymore, and I decided the information she gave me about her old art teacher, Champion, could prove to be very helpful.

Chapter Eleven

I hung my new *Banjo in a Garden* painting in our break-fast nook area and stood back to admire it. Somehow, banjos and sunflowers send out a happy, carefree message. I thought it would be a good way to start each day—eating breakfast while gazing at the cheery scene.

When Craig came home from work, I led him through the kitchen to show him my new art purchase.

"How do you like it?" I asked.

He studied it for a moment, then gave a nod of approval. "I like it. Like I always say, you can never go wrong with banjos. Where'd you get it?"

"Check out the signature," I said.

He stepped up to the painting and squinted to read the tiny print in the lower right corner. "Raven Covina? Isn't she the one—"

"Yep. She's the mistress who caused all the delays on the sale of Rancho Costa Little."

Craig scratched his head and stood back again, to look at the painting from a distance. "She's an artist?"

"Yes, and she's very good," I replied.

"I'd have to agree. How'd you get the painting?"

"I went to see her today. She's quite a unique character." I could see Craig's face fill with concern.

"I thought you were going to drop this," he said.

"I can't. You know how I am."

He smiled and wrapped his arms around me. "I know. So, you think Raven's the murderer? Did she paint the purple landscape?"

"I don't think so. But she told me about a teacher she had at college who made all his students mix their own paints for one of his classes. I thought I'd go talk to him tomorrow. Maybe he can give me some clues."

Craig stepped back and pulled an apple from the fruit basket on the table. "What does Sam think about you doing all this investigative work?" he asked, wiping the apple on his shirt.

"What he doesn't know won't hurt him," I said.

"Are you sure? I don't want you spending any more nights in jail because you made him mad," Craig reminded me.

"He won't. We're buddies now. He even suggested I get my private investigator's license so he could cut me more slack."

"More slack? He already puts up with more of your—"

I shot him my be-careful-where-you're-going-with-this-statement look. He started over.

"He already gives you a lot of leeway. You're not considering getting your license, are you?"

I shook my head. "No. I have no desire to become a private investigator."

He gave me his oh-really look, and we both broke into laughter.

I decided I'd try to talk to Bridgett Winnomore before I went to see Champion. She was the only person I hadn't talked to yet, involving the sale of Lou's house. I drove by the address Chuck gave me to scope it out, then I parked at the curb.

She lived in a duplex in an area mostly populated with college students. A boy about the age of twelve played by himself in the front yard. He had a baseball and glove and one of those big nets that return the ball to you when you throw one at it. He threw the ball hard, as though he were angry. I figured the boy was Bridgett's son, and he probably had every right to be angry, considering the bad things that had happened in his family in the past year.

I'd spent hours trying to come up with a role to play in order to talk to Bridgett and get information from her. I figured that Sam had already questioned her, so I decided I'd just be honest and straightforward. She'd either talk to me, or she wouldn't.

I got out of my car and stood for a moment on the sidewalk, watching the boy try to rip apart the throwback net with his fastball. He noticed me looking, but ignored my stare. If anything, he seemed even more determined to destroy the net with each throw.

Finally, I took a step up the walk toward the duplex and spoke to him. "Hi. Is this your house?"

He threw the ball one more time, then held it in his

glove. He glared at me through angry eyes, then nodded slightly.

"Is that a yes or a signal for a curveball?" I asked, smiling.

He softened his glare. I think I might even have detected a grin. "Yeah. I live here."

"Is your mom home?"

He looked me up and down before he answered. He wasn't a very trusting soul, for good reason. "She's inside," he finally said, then returned to his game.

Bridgett Winnomore answered the door with a phone stuck between her ear and shoulder, and a textbook held open against her hip, which seemed to be acting as her bookmark. She was pleading into the phone as she signaled for me to wait.

"I need the night off because I have a big test tomorrow and I have to study," she explained to whoever was on the other end of the phone line.

"But if I fail this test, I have to take the class over again next semester," she pleaded. "I won't be able to graduate."

I watched her eyes swell up with tears as she listened to the reply. Then I saw the same anger in her face that I saw in the little boy throwing balls in the yard. "I'm not coming to work tonight, Abbey. Fire me if you have to, but becoming a nurse is more important to me than waiting tables in your lousy restaurant." She held the phone out in front of her face and used her thumb to press the button to end the call. Then she looked at me, a total stranger standing on her front porch. "What?" she blurted.

I could tell her morning was not going well at all. I didn't want to make it any worse. "Are you Bridgett Winnomore?" I asked.

She gave me the same suspicious glare that Uncle Rupert used to give me after he found out I hid behind the garage to watch him hide Easter eggs before our annual family picnic. I was only five at the time, but even to this day, he makes one of the little kids guard me while he performs his yearly egg-hiding task.

Bridgett's face turned from angry to concerned. "Are you from Scott's school?" she asked.

"No. I bought your father-in-law's house, and I just wondered if you had time to talk?"

She let out a sigh of relief. I got the feeling Scott was the boy in the yard, and he must be having trouble at school.

She transferred the heavy textbook to her other hip. "I really have to study for this test—"

"I won't take up much of your time," I assured her.

She peered around me at her son playing in the yard. "Scotty! Ten more minutes, then I want you in the house to finish your homework."

He barely acknowledged her request, and I wondered if he'd obey her or defiantly throw that ball until midnight.

"Ten minutes," she finally said to me as she pushed open the screen door to let me in.

Her living space was small and there were books and papers stacked everywhere. A sink full of dishes piled higher than the faucet, threatened to tip over at the slightest movement. A line of ants had made a trail across the kitchen floor to a glob of what looked like strawberry jam. She grimaced as she stepped over the busy line of insects.

"Darn that boy. I told him to wipe up his mess," she complained as she searched for a roll of paper towels buried under a collection of shabby old dishrags. She rummaged under the sink for a bottle of spray cleaner as she talked. "What did you want to talk about? Is there a problem with the house? Because if there is, you're asking the wrong person."

"No, no. There's no problem with the house. Has Detective Wright been here to talk to you yet?" I asked.

She sprayed the entire line of ants with 409 cleaner, then wiped them up, along with the jam. "Are you from the police?" she asked.

"No. Detective Wright is a friend of mine, and he's working on this investigation at my request."

"You mean about Lou being murdered?"

"So he was here?"

She cleared a spot on the kitchen table and motioned for me to sit down. She took the seat opposite me. "He came by last night. I feel just awful about poor Lou. I always liked him. I felt so bad after my mother-in-law died that I told Joey we ought to have him move in with us. He was so lonely."

I studied her face. She seemed sincere. "You don't know who gave him the painting he had hanging in his living room, do you? The purple one?"

"Detective Wright asked me the same question. I've racked my brain, but I don't think he ever told us where he got it."

I frowned and stared at the big textbook she'd been carrying around with her. "Are you a nursing student?"

"Yes. It's a lot tougher than I thought it'd be. I'm trying

to pass my classes, work a lousy job that barely earns enough to make ends meet, and keep my kid from becoming a juvenile delinquent. I'll be lucky if I don't commit . . ."

I waited for her to finish. Murder? Suicide? What was she capable of, I wondered. She never did finish the sentence. I finally broke the silence. "You don't think your boss would actually fire you for not working tonight, would she?"

Bridgett let out a cynical laugh. "Don't ever work for a spoiled, self-centered woman," she said. "I've never been exposed to a more inconsiderate, back-biting, evil person in my entire life, and that includes my two-timing husband. Late husband," she added.

"So you think she really might fire you?"

"Abbey? Oh, without a doubt. But you know what? I don't care. I'll find another lousy job that doesn't pay enough, and probably hate it as much as this one, but I'm graduating soon, and then things are going to change. Scotty and me will move out to the country, and I'll have more time to spend with him. And I'll finally make enough money to buy a decent car that doesn't break down every other week."

I could see Bridgett was determined to reach her goal, and I had no doubt that she'd make it. Like her son, she'd been through a lot and was toughened by her experiences. "When do you graduate?" I asked.

"This is my last semester—if I pass all my classes, that is. I'm getting it done faster than most of the others. A friend of mine in the program took a bunch of silly electives the first year, so she has another semester before she can graduate. Of course, she's still living at home, so there's no pressure for her to hurry."

"Electives? Like art?" I asked.

"Yeah. You know. Music appreciation, pottery making—classes you take *after* you're burnt out from twenty years of nursing and want something to relax you."

"Did you ever take any classes from Mister Champion?" I asked.

"The art teacher? Yeah, I think I took one back when I was trying to get all my prerequisites in. I needed to round out my units, and I couldn't take anything heavy. Basket weaving or some silly thing like that."

"No painting classes?"

She gave me that suspicious look, again. "You're wondering if I killed my father-in-law."

"I'm wondering *who* killed your father-in-law. Maybe somebody you know from school who also knew Lou. Can you think of anyone like that?"

Bridgett pushed her chair away from the table and peered out the window at Scott, who was still throwing the ball, only now he had a friend to catch it instead of the net. She pushed the screen door open and called him into the house. "Come on, Scotty. Time's up."

She turned to me. "I don't know anyone who would have killed Lou. If you don't mind, I have to study," she said, holding the screen door open for me to leave.

On my way out, I stopped on the porch and rummaged through my purse for a pen and a scrap of paper. I scrawled some information on it and handed it to Bridgett. "This is my name and the number for the King Rooster Bar and Grill, over by the marina. Gary's the manager," I said, pointing to his name and number. "He's a great guy to work for, and I heard he's looking for a waitress. Tell him I sent you. He pays okay, and the tips are great."

Bridgett stared at the paper in her hand, then at me. "Thanks," she said, a little sheepishly.

I walked out the door and passed Scotty on his way in the house.

Bridgett called to me when I was halfway to my car. "I would help if I could. I really don't know any more than I already told you."

I smiled and nodded, then walked to my car. If Bridgett had a million dollars in cash, I doubt she'd still be here, slaving to get through school and working for the wicked witch so she could pay her bills.

Chapter Twelve

When I walked into Champion's classroom, my chin nearly hit the floor. Thirty art students each stood in front of their easels, working on the same image: a purple, monotone landscape—exactly the same one I'd taken off Lou Winnomore's wall. A framed print hung on the wall in the front of the class to serve as a guide. That must have been one of the prints that Eric at the police lab told me about.

I wandered around the classroom, searching for the man in charge. I found him helping a young woman who seemed to be having a difficult time with her paintbrush.

"You've got enough paint on your brush to cover my entire house. That's your problem," he explained. The young girl blushed with embarrassment, then helplessly handed him the brush.

"Can you show me?" she drawled, with a southern accent so thick I halfway expected to see a crate of Georgia peaches under her hoop skirt—if she were wearing one, that is.

I remembered Raven's comment that Champion was attractive. "Cute" was the word she used, as I recall. I watched him charm her as he took young Scarlett's hand and moved it back and forth across her pallet to remove the excess paint. I fully expected her to swoon. He had deep-set brown eyes and a strong jaw. When he smiled, a dimple formed in his cheek and I swear I saw a sparkle from his teeth, like one of those toothpaste commercials. He stood six-foot-four, easily, and was built like an Olympic swimmer. He wore faded jeans, a plaid shirt with the sleeves rolled up to just below his elbows, and leather boots. My first impression was that he belonged on the front porch of a rustic, Rocky Mountain log cabin, with a guitar in his lap and a good dog at his feet.

When he finally had his helpless student's overloaded paintbrush crisis under control, he looked up to see me, a stranger, in his classroom.

"Can I help you?" he asked.

I cleared my throat and offered my hand. "Hello, Mister Champion. My name is Devonie. I wondered if I could have a few minutes of your time."

At that very moment, a voice from a distant corner cried out in a pathetic whine. "Mister Champion. I need your help. Please?"

He gave me the look of a fireman being summoned to rescue a woman from a burning building. "Be right back," he said, flashing me a movie-star grin that I'm sure kept many women waiting for his return.

I waved my hand. "That's okay. I'll wait till your class is over. I'm sure they need you more than me."

He smiled and checked his watch. "Fifteen minutes," he said, then rushed off to save his young pupil.

I strolled around the classroom, admiring the work of the fledgling artists. Some definitely had more talent than others. Most of the students were young women, and if I had to guess, were only there because Champion was teaching the class. He could have been teaching primitive spear making, and they'd have signed up.

After the class ended, and Champion helped the last of the needy students with their heavy easels, he offered me a chair near his desk.

"How can I help you?" he asked again.

"Well, I don't really know where to begin," I started.

"Did you want to sign up for a class? I don't know if I have room, but let me check my—"

"No. I'm here because I understand you teach a class that requires the students to mix their own dry pigments into specific mediums."

"Right. That's this class. You sure you don't want to sign up?"

"No, at least not this semester. I'm curious about this landscape you use," I said, pointing to the framed print hanging on the wall. "I noticed all your students were copying it."

He gazed at the picture. "Right. It's the first assignment for the class. I like the simplicity of the lines and the use of one base color. It gives the students a feel for mixing tones without having to worry about complex lines or keeping proportions accurate," he explained.

"So you use this same assignment to start the class each time it's offered?"

"Yes. It's a very effective teaching tool," he said.

"For how long?"

"How long have I been teaching?"

"How long have you used that print to teach this class?"

Champion's smile turned to a frown. He eyed me with suspicion. "You're not a lawyer, are you? Because I only use this as a tool. None of my students ever sign their work on this assignment. I make sure they don't. Like I say, it's just an exercise."

I shook my head and waved my hands in a motion to tell him to relax. "No. I'm not a lawyer. I'm not worried about any copyright infringements. I just found one of these paintings in a house I bought, and I wondered who painted it."

Champion relaxed. "Good. You had me worried for a minute. You found an unsigned original?"

"Yes. It had to have been one of your students' work, now that I see what you're doing here."

"Most likely. But I've been using that print for years, and this class is always full. I don't know how you'd ever be able to tell which student painted it."

"How many years?" I asked.

"Gosh, it must be fifteen years. And I teach it every quarter. At least thirty students in each class. If you do the math, that's a lot of possibilities."

I cringed as I tried to calculate the number in my head.

"That's about eighteen hundred," he announced.

I gave him my most pleading expression. "I don't suppose if I showed it to you, you could remember who painted it?"

He laughed. "You're kidding, right? Besides the fact that most of them look almost exactly the same, I can barely remember who was in my class tonight, let alone fifteen years ago."

I'm sure several dozen hearts would break if they'd heard him admit he doesn't remember them.

"Why do you want to know who the artist is? I'm sure any one of these students would be happy to give you another, if that's what you're after. Most of them give the assignment away after it's complete and graded anyway."

Part of me felt I'd just stumbled onto a huge clue that should put me infinitely closer to finding out who killed Lou Winnomore. Only problem was I didn't have the resources to track down nearly two thousand alumni, even if I thought I could get their names.

"You don't happen to recall a student named Raven Covina, do you?" I asked.

"Ah, young Miss Raven. Now there's a student that's hard to forget," he replied, gazing into space as though he were re-living a pleasant experience.

"She took this class?"

"She certainly did."

"Then she would have painted this assignment?"

"Yes, but she's not the artist you're looking for."

"She's not? How could you know that?"

"Because she gave the painting to me," he explained, still wearing the silly grin of a schoolboy in love.

I noticed the gold wedding band on Champion's left hand. A married man—just Raven's type, if she really was the home-wrecker everyone said. He must have noticed me staring at his hand.

"Raven was the most talented artist I'd seen come through here in my entire career. I tried to encourage her to pursue her art with more seriousness. She's a funny girl. You know her?"

I nodded. "We just met. I bought one of her paintings, as a matter of fact."

A broad smile spread across his face. "That's great. So she's finally selling her work?"

"At least one. I tried to prod her in that direction too. Such a waste to let those paintings sit, unseen, in her spare room."

Champion nodded in agreement.

"So you still have her purple painting?" I asked.

"No. I gave it to a friend who moved into a new apartment and needed something to cover a big hole he put in the wall."

There was no telling how many of these paintings were floating around, and just how many times they'd been given away.

"How about Bridgett Winnomore? Do you recall her in any of your classes?" I asked.

He searched his memory, then finally shook his head. "Can't say that I recall that name."

Right. Raven Covina is the kind of woman men cheat on their wives with. There's something unforgettable about her. Bridgett, on the other hand, is the kind of woman who gets cheated on. As a wife, it doesn't pay to be forgettable, but as a murderer, maybe it does. Maybe Bridgett really was in one of his classes, but unlike Raven, she failed to make an everlasting impression.

I thanked Champion for his help and wandered back to my car, wondering what to do next.

Sam Wright was barking into his phone about the ludicrous state of the judicial system when I walked into his office. He nodded at me as I pushed the door closed and strolled over to his new whiteboard. As he continued to reprimand whoever was on the other end of the line, I picked up a marker and pulled the cap off. Sam quickly put his hand over the phone's mouthpiece. "Hey. What do you think you're doing?" he asked me, ignoring the caller.

"I'm adding a clue to the list," I explained as I began writing on his precious board.

Sam removed his hand from the phone. "Call me back when you've grown a new brain, Huey!" he roared, then slammed the phone down on its cradle.

I jumped at the sound. "My goodness. Who was that?" I asked, surprised at his anger.

"Another defense attorney who wants to suppress evidence that would, with a doubt, convict his client," Sam said, fuming.

"On what grounds?" I asked.

"The kid confessed and handed us the murder weapon, but his brilliant lawyer says we can't use either because the kid's got a hearing problem and may not have heard us read him his rights."

"That's ridiculous."

"I know. Welcome to our wonderful judicial system. Anyhow, what's this clue you have?"

"Our killer was a student at UCSD sometime in the past fifteen years or so."

"That doesn't narrow it down very much," he replied.

"Wait. I'm not finished. He took a class called Principals of Color. Every student in the class is required to paint the same purple landscape I found in Lou's house, and they're also required to mix their own paints for the assignment."

Sam rubbed his chin with the back of his hand and watched me scribble on his board. "How'd you find this out?"

"I spoke with the teacher. His name's Peter Champion." I finished writing and put the marker back in its tray. "I'm not going to write this down, but if I had to make a bet, I'd say our killer is female."

Sam crossed his arms over his broad chest and studied my face. "Now what makes you say that?"

"It's just a hunch, really. Close to seventy percent of Champion's students today were women. If that's typical for all his classes, then the odds are in my favor that I'm right."

Sam pushed his chair back and pulled a bundle of paper out of his file cabinet. He slid it across his desk toward me. "These are recent statistics from the Department of Justice. Take a look and you'll see that men are almost nine times more likely to commit murder than women."

I studied the charts and graphs, then I shoved it back toward him. "But look there, where it shows that woman are more likely to use poison than any other means when they do commit murder," I rebutted.

Sam glanced at the chart briefly, then jammed it back into his file cabinet. "All I'm saying is, if you're going to go on hunches or odds, then the percentages point to a male offender."

"I'd agree if the weapon were anything other than poison. I bet I'm right."

Sam smiled and shook his head, giving me a doubtful look.

"Okay, I'll make you a bet. If our killer turns out to be female, you owe me . . . what? What can you afford, Mister Cheapo?"

"Cheapo? I'm not cheap. I'm just thrifty," he replied, defending his character.

"Fine, Mister Thrifty. If I win, you owe Craig and I the biggest, best dinner to be found in San Diego. If you win, which you won't, Craig and I will take you out on the *Plan C* for a weekend of fishing. Deal?"

Sam grinned from one overconfident ear to the other. "You're on, Miss Know-it-All. What's that teacher's name, again?"

"Peter Champion. Why?"

"I'm going over to the university and gonna get a list of his past students."

I got up and headed for the door. "Good. While you're doing that, I'm going to call around and find out who has the most expensive lobster in town."

Chapter Thirteen

Fiona invited me to play cards with her lady investors' club, and since Craig had to stay late at the hospital for a staff meeting, I agreed to join in. It was going to be sort of a girls' night out and I looked forward to it.

Fiona answered the door in top form, wearing a long, red evening gown with matching shoes and a feathery black hat. She wore black velvet gloves that went all the way up past her elbows. I gaped at her attire only long enough for her to grab my hand and yank me into the house.

"Devonie! You made it!" She led me to the dining room, where a group of woman sat around the table, drinking margaritas and showing off their jewelry. They were all dressed for a formal affair and looked as though they'd spent the entire day in the capable hands of a professional hairdresser.

"Girls, this is Devonie. She just bought that little estate sale house I had listed. If we're all real nice to her, she might join our little investors' club," Fiona announced, as she paraded me around the table like a poodle in a dog show.

All the ladies stopped their oohing and aahing and looked me over. Now I really felt like a dog in a contest. Fiona didn't tell me to dress as though I were attending the Oscars. I'd put on my most comfortable jeans and sneakers, and because it was a little bit cool outside, found a sweatshirt without a stain on the front. This is how I thought people dressed to play cards. Hopefully, this would be my only faux pas of the evening.

Finally, one of the ladies broke the silence. "You have the most beautiful eyes I've ever seen," she said to me. "That shirt you're wearing brings the color out so vividly." Then they all nodded and agreed with her, smiling and greeting me with the most gracious hospitality that I nearly forgot how under-dressed I was. One of the ladies patted the empty seat next to hers and invited me to sit.

Fiona disappeared into the kitchen for a moment then returned with a tray of chips and salsa and a margarita. "Okay, everyone knows Devonie's name, so now you all tell her yours," she said, placing the drink in front of me.

The woman to my immediate left started the show. I guessed her age to be somewhere around the same as Fiona's. Her hair was colored an almost unnatural red, and she wore a forest-green evening gown. A huge diamond sat perched on her finger like a finch. "I'm Dorothy," she said.

"Dorothy owns five duplexes and a triplex. I sold her every one of them," Fiona boasted, taking a seat across from me.

Next to Dorothy was a younger woman, maybe closer to my age. She wore a basic black dress with spaghetti straps and a delicate pearl necklace. "Hi. I'm Melissa," she said, with a kind smile.

"Melissa and her husband buy and sell rehab houses, like you're doing," Fiona added. She picked up a huge stack of cards and began shuffling.

Between Melissa and Fiona sat the most striking woman in the room. She looked like an Italian movie star from my mother's era. Her thick black hair fell down both sides of her face in even waves, like frosting on a cake. I've always wondered how women make hair do that—without lacquer. She wore a turquoise dress with a matching feather boa. She also wore at least one ring on every finger, and even two on her thumbs. I wondered how she'd be able to hold her cards. "Pleased to meet you, Devonie. My name's Sophia, but everyone calls me Sophie."

I smiled and waited for Fiona to describe her real estate portfolio, but she was too busy shuffling that enormous stack of cards in front of her. There must have been six decks. "What kind of investing do you do, Sophie?" I asked.

"I own an apartment complex. It's small, but it keeps me living the lifestyle I've become accustomed to."

I stared at Sophie for a moment and wondered if she might actually be that actress from days gone by.

"And I'm Millie," the tiny woman in the seat to my right announced. She was the most petite thing, and I wondered where in the world she could find an evening gown in a size one. "I'm a general contractor," she said.

"You? But you're so tiny," I marveled.

She stuck her chin out, pulled up her chiffon sleeve and made an attempt to flex her bicep muscle. "Don't let these little chicken wings fool you. I'm tough as steel," she said. The entire group broke out laughing.

Fiona continued cutting the cards. "Millie is a general contractor by trade, but she hires subs to do everything but the decorating. She's the smartest woman I know. After her husband passed away, she studied for the state licensing exam and passed with flying colors."

I gave her a smile appropriate for how impressed I was. Then I turned to Fiona. "Why didn't you tell me the dress code? I feel like I should be sitting in the kitchen with the maid."

"Oh, nonsense. I didn't think you'd come if I told you we crazy old broads dress up like a bunch of floozies for our monthly game of Spite and Malice. You can dress up next time if you decide to join."

Millie took a swig of her margarita and wiped the salt from the edges of her mouth. "Come on, Fiona. Deal the cards," she said, anxious to get started.

I held up my hand. "Wait a minute. I thought we were playing poker or blackjack. I don't know how to play . . . what's it called?"

"Spite and Malice. It's easy," Fiona said. "We'll play a practice round to show you."

As the evening rolled on, it became clear to me that these women didn't care who won or lost. Tonight was a night of dress-up and socializing. Nothing more. Dorothy kept insisting that no one let their hands be seen by any of the other players, yet consistently announced the cards she drew from the pile on the table, as they were so useless to her that she'd never have a chance of winning.

Millie kept bending the rules to allow me to take back plays that were not in my best interest. No one seemed to mind. The fact that there was no money on the table probably had a great deal to do with their agreeable temperament.

Fiona dealt the next hand. "Did I tell you girls that Devonie found a lottery ticket worth millions in that little house I sold her?"

The women nearly choked on their chips and gaped at me. "What?" they all said in unison.

Fiona continued dealing. "But someone stole it. Turns out that poor man who owned the house was murdered, probably for the ticket. How's the investigation going, toots?"

Everyone's eyes were on me. I straightened my cards on the table and took another sip of my margarita. They weren't letting me off the hook until I spilled the beans. "Sam hasn't made any arrests yet."

Millie gasped and put her hand over her mouth. "Oh my. Murder? How exciting. Tell us more. Maybe we can help solve it."

"I really don't think we should talk about it. I mean, it's still an ongoing investigation," I said, hoping she'd drop the subject. I should have realized that once the cat was out of the bag, there'd be no putting it back without some serious scratches on my arms.

"Oh, I'm sorry," Fiona said. "You're right, of course. You can't talk about the details, toots."

I was finally able to breathe again, and relaxed my fists to allow my fingernails to dislodge from my palms.

"But everyone already knows that Arthur Simon got that

lottery ticket. It was all over the news," Fiona blurted, before I could stop her.

I cringed as soon as I heard her say his name. I thought Millie was going to explode. "Arthur Simon murdered him?" she gasped.

I shook my head frantically. "No! No! Arthur Simon didn't have anything to do with it. Please, Fiona. We really shouldn't be talking about it."

Fiona frowned. "I'm sorry, toots. It's just that it was all over the news and all, how Arty won that money. And it had to be the ticket you found in that little house. I mean, it was for fifty-eight million, just like yours, and it was just about to expire."

Fiona couldn't help herself. The women around the table were eating this up like chocolate-covered strawberries. I wanted to slide under the table and disappear. Sam would kill me if he knew what was going on.

"Fifty-eight million? My God! How did Arthur get the ticket if he wasn't the murderer?" Dorothy asked.

"Please, ladies. Arthur Simon is not a murderer. This whole conversation should not be taking place," I pleaded. "Fiona, can we just play the game?"

Fiona gave me a sympathetic smile. "Sure, toots. We won't say another word, will we girls?"

They all pretended to lock their lips and throw the imaginary keys over their shoulders.

"I'm sorry. It's just that I could get in a lot of trouble if Sam—"

Fiona shushed me. "Don't you be sorry, toots. We all understand. Now let's play."

"Thank you," I squeaked.

Fiona played her hand and swallowed the last of her margarita.

"Didn't you used to date Arthur Simon, Fiona?" Dorothy piped up.

"Just the one time, but I've been trying to get in touch with him, ever since he—"

Fiona spotted my glare and stopped herself. "Just one time, Dorothy. Now I think we better concentrate on the game."

Not another word was spoken about Arthur Simon or the lottery ticket or the murder for the rest of the evening. At the end of the night, the group invited me back to the next monthly game. I promised I would attend, although it would mean I'd have to shop for a suitable outfit. I wondered if my wedding dress would do.

Chapter Fourteen

I'd just sent Craig off to work, and was about to head over to Rancho Costa Little to see if I could do some yard cleanup since Sam wouldn't let me remove anything else from the house until he completed his investigation. I grabbed my keys and was headed for the garage when I heard tires screech in the driveway. Seconds later, someone was pounding violently on the front door. I hurried over to the window and peeked out to see Sam banging with one hand and holding a newspaper with the other.

"I'm coming! Settle down!" I hollered through the door, before he busted it down. Once I'd opened it an inch, he shoved his way in and slammed the door behind him.

"What have you done?" he demanded, waving the paper in my face.

I stared blankly at him, unsure what to say. "I haven't done anything. What's wrong?"

Sam's face was beet-red and his chest heaved with every breath. He slapped the newspaper down on the table and jammed his finger on a spot on the front page. "Read this," he ordered.

I read the headline and immediately realized why he was furious. It read: SIMON CLAIMS MURDER VICTIM'S PRIZE.

"Don't tell me you don't know anything about this," he said, pointing an accusing finger at me.

I read the story, which confirmed the fact that Lou Winnomore had indeed been murdered, and the motive was believed to be for the winning lottery ticket.

"I didn't do this. I swear. Why would I?" I insisted.

"Then who did?" he boomed, still seething.

I melted into a chair and rubbed my temples to ward off an impending headache. "I might have an idea," I admitted, squeezing my eyes shut and cringing at the anticipation of his reaction.

"I knew it! I swear this is the last time I let you get involved in an investigation. I don't know what I was thinking," he hissed.

"Now wait a minute. Just because I think I might know who's responsible for the story doesn't mean I had anything to do with it."

Sam opened his mouth to protest, but I cut him off.

"And besides, there wouldn't even be an investigation if it weren't for me. Don't you forget that."

Sam stood in the middle of the room with his arms folded across his big chest, glaring at me. I picked up the phone next to the chair and dialed Fiona's number.

As I suspected, the conversation at last night's game led to the story on the front page. Dorothy's son is a reporter for the *Union Tribune*. Dorothy must have left the card game last night and went directly to his house to give him the scoop. I explained to Sam the events of last evening. He didn't cool down much, but at least his hostility was transferred from me to Fiona and her cronies.

"So, what does this mean to the investigation?" I asked, already pretty sure what the answer would be.

"Up till now, it looked like the killer was sticking around town. This story might scare him off. He's got a million bucks to play with. He can go just about anywhere."

"She," I corrected.

"Whatever. The point is, we no longer have the luxury of time to figure this one out. It may already be too late."

"I'm not sure we ever really did have the luxury of time." I spotted a cufflink under the coffee table that Craig had lost a few nights ago. We'd searched the entire house, and there it was, in plain view. I picked it up and stared at it, dumbfounded at how we could have missed it. "Why don't we go back over to the house and look again. Maybe we've missed something," I suggested.

Sam nodded. "At this point, that's about all we can do. I'll follow you over."

I dumped the contents of one of the big plastic garbage bags onto the garage floor. Sam had already been through the bags once, the first time he searched the house, but we had more information now. Maybe something would stand out this time around. Sam and I sifted through every scrap of paper or bit of miscellaneous trash, looking for something we might have missed.

"Did your guys ever come up with anything on the e-mail message sent to Arthur Simon?" I asked as I gingerly unfolded a slimy, disgusting piece of paper that turned out to be a grocery store receipt.

"No luck. This guy really covered his tracks."

I frowned as I picked out another gooey bit of trash from the pile. "Did you get the class list from the university?"

"Got it. Sixteen-hundred-and-forty-eight students. I've got my guys crosschecking it with students from classes that have access to cyanide in their lab work."

Sam grimaced as he pulled an old, black banana peel out of the heap. He tossed it aside.

We'd separated the items that didn't seem totally without worth into categories. Receipts went into one stack, notes and lists into another, bills and correspondence into a third. Anything that didn't fall into any of those categories went into a miscellaneous pile.

By the time noon rolled around, I was ready to get up off that hard concrete floor and regain some circulation in my lower half. "You hungry?" I asked.

"I was, until I found that moldy sardine sandwich," he replied, nodding toward the heap of useless trash in the corner.

I headed for the door. "Well, I'm starving. There's a little grocery store around the corner. I'll get some drinks and stuff to make sandwiches. What do you want?"

"Anything but fish," Sam said as he struggled to get to his feet. "I'll stay here and keep working."

I walked into the quaint little Ma and Pa grocery store and smiled at the sound of the clanking cowbell hanging on the door. I recalled from a news report that this was the store where the winning lottery ticket had originally been purchased. I grabbed a basket from a stack near the entrance and searched the aisles for bread, mayonnaise, and plastic forks and knives. I found fruit juices in the cooler, and to my amazement, the little store boasted a full deli. I added sliced turkey, ham and provolone cheese to my basket and grabbed a head of romaine lettuce from the produce section.

The tiny store had two cash registers, but only one was open. A large, bald-headed man wearing a green apron stood behind the counter, putting groceries into a bag for his customer. I stepped to the back of the line and waited, enjoying the smells of the produce and the fresh bread that had just been delivered.

"Thanks, Margie," the big man said as he handed the little old lady her bag of groceries. "You need help out with that?"

Margie's bony hand shook as she grasped the handle of the bag. She smiled and waved him off. "No thank you, Otis. I can manage."

Before Otis could help the next customer in line, a bell rang from somewhere in the back of the store. Otis stretched as high as he could to see who was at the back counter. The bell rang again. "Be right with you!" he hollered to the impatient customer.

"I just want to buy a lottery ticket," a voice called back from a distant corner of the market.

The man in line in front of me placed his groceries on the belt and gave Otis a sympathetic smile. "Hey, Otis. You a one-man show today?"

The counter bell rang again. Otis clenched his teeth. "I said I'd be right there!"

"I'm sort of in a hurry," the impatient voice called back.

Otis' customer stretched to see who the annoying man was, then turned back to Otis. "Go ahead and help that guy. I'm not in a hurry." Then the man turned and noticed I was in line behind him. "Oh, sorry. Maybe you are?"

I smiled and shook my head. "No. Go ahead and help him before he has a seizure."

Otis smiled. "Thanks, folks. I'll be right back. Sorry about this."

I set my basket on the floor while we waited for Otis to return. The customer in front of me whistled and gazed at the collection of tabloid papers stacked in a rack next to the checkout stand. "Look at that," he said, pointing to a hideous photo of a woman standing next to some alien creature. "Woman is visited by alien and loses fifty pounds overnight. Gee, and I thought diet and exercise were the only way to do that," the man said, chuckling. I laughed with him.

Otis rushed back through the aisles to get to the checkout stand. "Sorry about that."

"No problem. Where's Casey? Why are you all alone here today?" the customer asked.

I thought I could see steam coming from under Otis' collar. "Don't get me started," he said as he passed a can of corn across the UPC scanner.

"She have finals this week?" the customer pressed.

Otis shook his head. "Not that she told me. Had her on the schedule to open with me this morning, but she never showed up. Darn kid. If I weren't her father, I'd fire her. Maybe I will anyway."

"Can't you get someone to come in for the day to help you out?"

"Leslie's coming in at one. Mark went to lunch, but he'll be back soon. She couldn't have picked a worse day to be a no-show. I had deliveries this morning, and yesterday was government-check day, so we've been twice as busy as usual."

Another customer walked in and headed for the back of the store. Otis scowled at the man's back, waiting to see if he went toward the lottery ticket counter.

"Thanks, Steve," Otis said, handing the customer his change and receipt.

I placed my basket on the counter and gave Otis a sympathetic smile. "So Casey's your daughter?" I asked, politely.

"Not today she's not," he barked, grabbing the bread out of my basket and squashing it as he waved it across his scanner. I wondered if it would ever regain its original shape.

"I hope she's not sick," I said.

Otis snatched the mayonnaise from my basket. "She ain't sick. Saw her bright and early this morning, eating a bowl of oatmeal and reading the paper. *My* paper, as a matter of fact."

Otis took the last item from my basket and totaled my bill. "That'll be nineteen forty-six."

I handed him a twenty.

"You got the forty-six cents, by chance? I'm running short on change and I can't get to the bank until Leslie gets here."

I dug through my change purse and produced forty-six cents. Otis handed me a dollar bill and my receipt.

I put the change away and stared at the receipt while he bagged my groceries. The receipt looked the same as the ones I'd dug out of Lou Winnomore's trash. He probably shopped here regularly. It was close to home and convenient.

The counter bell at the back of the store rang again, and Otis rolled his eyes as he handed me my bag. "Thanks for being patient," he said. Then he rushed out from behind the counter and disappeared behind a stack of paper towels.

I started out the front door, then stopped. Something Chuck had said instantly replayed in my head. *You could wallpaper his house with that box full of all those tickets he bought.* Those were his exact words. I turned and went back into the store.

I wandered down an aisle to the back counter where Otis was busy selling another lottery ticket. When his customer left, he smiled at me. "Forget something?" he said.

"Yeah. I need a lottery ticket," I said.

"Quick pick?"

I nodded. "That's fine."

I placed the dollar bill on the counter as Otis handed me the ticket.

"Your daughter's a student at UCSD?" I asked, making small talk.

"Yeah. Probably the biggest waste of money I ever spent."

"Education's never a waste of money. What's her major?"

"Get this. Undeclared. Tell me what she's gonna do with that?" he replied, rolling his eyes.

I smiled politely and looked at the lottery ticket in my hand. "Well, I'm sure she'll think of something. Thanks again," I said, then headed back for the front of the store. Over the door was a large poster with Otis' smiling face beaming down on the customers. Under the picture, the caption read: OTIS BIGGSMUTH, YOUR FRIENDLY PROPRIETOR.

Otis Biggsmuth. Casey Biggsmuth. I made a mental note as I hurried out the door to my car. It took me less than two minutes to get back to the house, where I found Sam babbling to himself about rotten eggs and moldy cheese. I left him working in the garage.

I headed toward the back of the house. I re-checked every cupboard, every closet, every nook and cranny that might hold something I missed. I stood in the center of the master bedroom, perplexed. Then I pushed my way into the closet and stared at the ceiling. There it was—the access panel to the attic. I reached up, grabbed the string and pulled the spring-loaded panel down. A second string attached to a set of steps dangled within reach. I grabbed it and pulled. "Sam!" I shouted.

He came racing into the bedroom. "What?"

"I never checked the attic."

Moments later, I found myself crawling into a dark and dusty attic. I clicked on the flashlight Sam gave me and let it sweep across the sea of fluffy pink insulation and cobwebs. I found another string, this time to a light bulb in the rafters, and switched it on. A few plastic bags and boxes were stacked on a single sheet of plywood that had been set next to the access opening. I reached for them and handed them down to Sam, one by one. When I'd emptied the attic, I climbed back down the ladder. Sam had already begun rummaging through the boxes.

I tore open the plastic bags, but only found old sleeping bags. I knocked over a shoebox, causing the contents to fall out. Piles of papers, tied into small bundles with rubber bands littered the floor. I picked up a bundle and inspected it. "Look at this," I said.

It was a stack of lottery tickets. I gazed at the entire heap. There must have been hundreds of tickets. He picked up a stack. I leafed through them quickly, glancing at the dates and the numbers. They were all for Lou's same special numbers. My heart pounded a little faster. We gathered up all the tickets and put them back in the box, sorting them chronologically. There was a ticket for nearly every draw—two a week for the entire seven years.

I pulled the ticket I'd just bought from Otis out of my pocket and handed it to Sam. "I just bought this today, from the store where the winning ticket came from. Look at the store code, then look at the codes on all these tickets."

Sam took the ticket and studied it, then he filed through the newly discovered box of tickets. "He bought them all from the same place—like clockwork."

"It gets better," I said. "The owner's daughter works there. She's a student at UCSD, and she didn't show up for work this morning," I said, almost out of breath. "She read this morning's paper, then disappeared."

"You get her name?" he asked as he reached in his pocket for his cellphone.

"Casey. Her last name's probably Biggsmuth, same as her father."

Sam punched some numbers into his cellphone and waited for an answer. "Yeah. Johnson. You got that list of Champion's students?

"Check for Casey Biggsmuth, would you?"

Sam looked at me. "Spell it," he said.

I wrote it down on a piece of paper and handed it to him. He spelled it out for Johnson.

I paced the kitchen while we waited for an answer. It didn't take long, since Biggsmuth would have been near the top of the alphabetized list.

"Great! Put out an APB. Try to get a photo from the university. Get someone to the airport, the bus station, and I want someone at the border crossings. She's on the run."

Sam shoved his phone back in his pocket. "I'm going to that store to talk to her father."

I grabbed my purse and followed him out the door.

Otis Biggsmuth, for all he complained about his daughter, became her biggest advocate when it looked like she might be in trouble. He forced the police to get a warrant to search her room, which allowed her even more time to escape.

By the end of the day, with officers combing the airport, bus station, and the major border crossings, it looked like Casey Biggsmuth might have slipped through the cracks. She had a million dollars in cash, and a lot of incentive to stay away from San Diego.

Chapter Fifteen

I know Sam Wright, and when he gets his mind set on something, he's like a pitbull with its teeth clamped firmly on a mailman's leg. When the search of Casey's room didn't turn up any clues to where she might have gone, he obtained a warrant to search the entire Biggsmuth household. The crew started with the family's trash.

Sam called me the next day to give me the good news. A spunky new officer, eager to make a good impression, picked the tiniest piece of paper out of the mound of garbage and excitedly gave it to Sam. It was a deposit slip from a Mexican bank, with a branch right in Tijuana.

The bad news was that Sam didn't have any jurisdiction in Mexico. He couldn't legally cross the border to arrest Casey, but if she stepped one foot back into the United States, he'd have her behind bars faster than you can say "Tijuana Brass."

I munched on a carrot stick while I listened to Sam speculate on all the ways he could trap her, if only she'd come back.

"What if I could get her back here?" I said, halting his non-stop ranting in mid-sentence.

"I'll pretend I didn't hear that," he replied.

"I mean it. What if I could get her back here, to San Diego? Wouldn't that solve your problem?"

"Now you listen to me. I've had enough of your antics for a lifetime."

"I won't do anything crazy. You already owe Craig and me dinner. If I pull this off, we'll renegotiate the deal."

Sam didn't say anything for a long time. I wondered if he'd worked himself up into a stroke. "Sam? Are you there?"

"I don't want to know what you're up to, and if you get yourself into any trouble, don't expect me to bail you out," he finally said.

I smiled and took another bite of my carrot. "Don't worry. By this time next week, little Miss Casey will be safe and sound behind bars."

When I told Craig my plan, he didn't exactly jump on my bandwagon.

"Honey," I pleaded with him. "She killed that poor man and now she's gotten away with all that money. Someone has to stop her."

"What about Sam?" he suggested.

"He can't do anything as long as she's in Mexico. You know what it's like to get someone extradited, even if they're already in custody, which she isn't."

"But what if something goes wrong?"

"What could go wrong?"

"What could go wrong? You could wind up in jail, for one."

"Sam won't let that happen," I assured him.

"Wait a minute. Isn't Sam the one who put you in jail for interfering with an investigation? Have you forgotten?"

"He won't do that again," I said.

"He told you that?"

"Well, not in so many words, but you know how he is. Come on, Craig. She killed that man, and she's going to get away with it if we don't do something."

Not surprisingly, I couldn't even get Craig to support my plan. I'd just about given up, since I couldn't pull it off by myself. It wasn't until Sam's search of the Biggsmuth house turned up a ceramic mixing bowl and pestle with traces of cyanide on the surface that things changed. That was the clincher that proved Casey's guilt to Sam. He called me as soon as the lab results were in, and asked me to elaborate a little more on my plan to get Casey back to San Diego.

I didn't think Casey would go further than Tijuana, since it's close to home. I would have been surprised if she traveled as far as Mexico City or Puerto Rico. Even though she was a cold-blooded killer, she was also a nineteen-year-old girl who'd never lived anywhere but her parent's house.

I spent the next three days hanging out at a little sidewalk taco joint across the street from the bank in Tijuana where Casey made her last bank transaction. I sat under an umbrella and sipped bottled water I had stashed in my purse as I watched people come and go. I pretended to read a book or do crossword puzzles so I wouldn't look too conspicuous. When it felt like I'd spent enough time there, I'd move to another spot down the street. I kept alternating between locations that gave me a constant view of the front door of the bank.

After two days of people watching, I began to wonder if my plan was full of holes. Maybe Casey was more independent than I thought. Maybe she'd travel further south—Brazil, perhaps. Maybe she'd buy an airline ticket and get off the continent altogether. I started to doubt my instinct, but I told myself I'd stick it out till the end of the week. If she didn't show up by Friday, then I'd throw in the towel and admit defeat.

Finally, on the third day, an elf-like character with big, dark sunglasses and a baseball cap walked nervously into the bank. I launched myself out of my seat and hurried across the street. When she exited, I fell into step a few yards behind her. It was Casey. My luck was changing.

I followed her for miles. She walked in circles, sometimes. She was lost most of the time. She stopped to ask directions from a couple of locals, but it seemed her Spanish was not any better than their English. I worried that she'd notice me every time she turned around, but she was so intent on getting to wherever it was she was headed, she never even looked back.

When she finally found her destination, I had to reconsider just how lucky I really was. She'd walked into a car dealership. She must have made a withdrawal at the bank to buy a new car. If she bought a car and drove off the lot, I'd lose her. My car was parked somewhere miles away, near the bank, and I certainly couldn't run in and buy a new car myself, just to follow her.

I chewed my bottom lip and scanned the area. I spotted a couple of taxis parked a block away on the opposite side of the street. I jogged up the road and picked the one with the fewest dents. The driver was confused when I asked him to drive me to the car lot, which was only a block away. I asked him to wait there while I watched from the back seat as Casey shopped. She disappeared into the sales office. I was tempted to follow her inside, but I was afraid I might lose my taxi, so I waited. I figured she wouldn't be long, since she had cash and didn't have to wait for a credit approval.

As I expected, she soon bounced back out of the office with a set of keys in one hand and a huge smile painted across her face. She climbed into a shiny new Volkswagen. I was puzzled at her choice. She had a million dollars to play with. She could have bought a Mercedes or a Jaguar or any other extravagant automobile, but instead, she bought a bright green Bug.

As she pulled out of the dealership, I instructed my taxi driver to follow her. I hoped she'd know her way around the streets a little better than she did the sidewalks, otherwise, this cab ride could cost me a fortune. No such luck. I bet we passed the same street corner no less than five times looking for whatever it was she was after. "She lost," the taxi driver kept announcing over his shoulder and laughing, as the miles racked up on the meter.

"I know. Just keep following her," I urged him, as I peeked into my wallet to see how much cash I'd brought with me.

Casey finally landed at the Oasis Beach Resort. She pulled into the parking lot and searched for a spot far away from any other cars. While she eased up and down the aisles, I had the driver park and wait with the other cabs in front of the hotel. When Casey finally picked a spot and parked, I paid the driver and got out of the cab.

I watched her disappear into the resort's main lobby. I pulled my cellphone from my purse and dialed Craig's number.

"Okay, you're on," I said. "I'm at the Oasis Beach Resort. I'll meet you out front."

Within an hour, Craig and our co-conspirator pulled into the resort parking lot.

"Where's your car?" Craig asked me.

"I left it back near the bank. We can get it later. She's staying here, so I think our plan will work perfectly."

Peter Champion parked his car next to Craig's and stepped out. He gazed at the surroundings. He adjusted the ball cap on his head and grinned at me. "Baby Bear has landed," he said with a wink.

"Baby Bear?" I asked, puzzled.

He and Craig exchanged amused glances.

"That's his code name. You're Mama Bear, I'm Papa Bear, and he's—"

"Baby Bear. Clever. And I suppose Casey's Goldilocks?"

"I told you she'd catch on," Craig said to Peter. "She's a pro at this kind of stuff."

I scoffed at them both. "You call Sam?"

"Right before we left. He's up to speed," Craig answered.

"Did he say anything?"

"Just to remember that officially, he has nothing to do with this plan of yours, but unofficially, he's behind us all the way."

"Which means?"

"He'll bake us a cake with a file in it if we end up in prison," Peter replied, chuckling.

I chuckled along with him. "Didn't Craig tell you that Sam put me in jail once? For interfering with an investigation?"

The smile left Peter's face. "He did?"

Craig patted him on the back. "Not to worry, Peter. That was back before Sam got to know my lovely wife. She's grown on him now."

Peter forced a smile, but still seemed a little tense.

"Come on. We've got work to do," I said, taking Craig by the hand and leading him toward the hotel lobby. Peter followed.

We made our way to our two-room suite, where we quickly locked the door and spread out a map of the resort on a table. Craig pulled three walkie-talkies out of his sports bag and set them on the table next to the map.

"What are these for?" I asked, picking one up to inspect it.

"Communication," Craig answered.

"You don't think we'll look a little conspicuous? Three adults playing with walkie-talkies?" I said.

Craig scoffed. "Have you looked around? Every other person out there has a cellphone stuck to his ear half the time. We'll fit right in."

I could see there'd be no talking him out of these toys. I set the device back on the table and studied the map.

"Do we know what room she's in?" Peter asked.

"No. You stay here in the room, so she doesn't spot you before we're ready. Craig and I will wander around the place. She can't stay in her room forever. Chances are, she'll spend some time at the pool, or the beach, or the bar."

Craig made each of us take a walkie-talkie and test them before we left the room.

Craig checked the beach and the pool, describing every revealing bathing suit he saw to me over the walkie-talkie. I checked the restaurant and lounge.

"Mama Bear, this is Papa Bear. Do you read?" I heard Craig whisper over the walkie-talkie.

"What is it, Craig?" I replied.

"Papa Bear," he insisted.

I rolled my eyes and played along. "Okay, Papa Bear. What is it?"

"No sign of her. Let's meet at the appointed spot," he said.

We rendezvoused behind a group of palm trees in front of the hotel lobby. By six in the evening, neither of us had spotted her. "I'll let Peter know what's going on," I said as I held the walkie-talkie to my mouth.

"Okay. Then let's switch. You check the beach and pool, and I'll check inside," Craig said. "Let's meet back here in an hour."

"Okay."

I wandered around the pool and then strolled along the

beach. Thirty minutes later, the walkie-talkie squawked, then Craig's voice rang excitedly through the speaker.

"I have Goldilocks in sight. Looks like she's gonna sample some porridge," he said.

"She's going into the restaurant?" I asked.

"That's right. You ready Peter?"

"On my way," Peter answered.

Craig and I hunkered down behind a potted fern and watched Peter in action. He turned off his walkie-talkie and strolled into the restaurant.

Peter tipped the waiter $10 to seat him at a table directly in front of Casey's. She sat alone, sipping a colorful drink with a pineapple wedge and umbrella poking out the top. When he walked past her table, he made eye contact, then stopped in utter surprise.

We couldn't hear his words, but whatever he said seemed to be working its magic.

Casey gaped at him for a moment, then smiled and graciously offered him a seat at her table. He took her hand and held on to it as he sat next to her. The pair chatted and reminisced like they were old friends who hadn't seen each other for years. Come to think of it, that probably was exactly what they were—or maybe they'd been more than friends. Peter would never confess to being any more than her art teacher, but I had my suspicions.

"Man, he's smoother than a silk tie," Craig said as he strained to get a better view.

"I told you. You should see him with his students. I figured Casey would warm right up to him. She's here, all alone. She's probably scared. He's a familiar face—not threatening. And you're right, he's about as smooth as they come."

This is what I was counting on. Our plan was for Peter to get her to let her guard down. If she confessed to him that she was in some sort of trouble, he was to offer her a better hiding place on his sailboat. Even if she kept quiet about her predicament, he would invite her to go sailing with him for a couple of weeks. I'd given him some snapshots of the *Plan C* to show her. She'd have to know she'd be almost impossible to find out on the open ocean. I was pretty sure she'd take him up on his offer.

We watched Peter charm his prey, as we sat smugly in our hiding place, proud at how well the plan was working. He pulled the photographs out of his pocket and handed them to her, one by one. She seemed impressed. Great. We were to the point of inviting her to the boat. After about fifteen minutes, Casey excused herself, we assumed to go to the ladies room. Peter squeezed her hand briefly before she left, then relaxed and sat back in his seat, waiting for his new companion to return.

I checked my watch. Casey had been gone for five minutes. I wasn't too concerned. She was probably re-applying all her makeup, re-styling her hair, and triple-checking her outfit. I could see the sign for the restrooms from my position. I stood up. "I'm just gonna go check on her," I said.

Craig nodded, but kept watching Peter.

When I walked into the restroom, it was empty. I rushed back out and tried to spot her. The only way for her to get past us was if she'd gone out through the kitchen, rather than through the dining room. I raced through the kitchen and out to the parking lot. I spotted Casey throwing a bag into her car and hopping into the driver's seat.

I grabbed the walkie-talkie. "Papa Bear! This is Mama Bear! Goldilocks has flown the coop! I repeat, she's on the run!"

I raced to Craig's car and reached it just as he came blasting out of the hotel. I pulled my set of keys from my purse and jumped into the driver's side. He darted across the parking lot and jumped into the passenger seat just as I was pulling out of the parking spot.

"Where is she?" he asked, out of breath.

I pointed to the red taillights that were just disappearing around the corner. "Over there, in the green Volkswagen."

I punched the accelerator and headed for the parking lot exit. A string of cars kept me from pulling out onto the main drag. "Come on, come on, come on," I chanted, trying to will the traffic to cooperate. Finally, a red light stopped the traffic, and I squealed the tires as I sped out onto the boulevard.

"Can you see her?" I asked, scanning the road ahead.

"No. She's too far ahead of us," Craig said, straining to see in the dark.

I drove to the next signal and waited at the red light. "I wonder what spooked her?" I said, impatiently drumming the steering wheel with my thumbs. I peered out all the windows trying to spot the little green Bug.

"I don't know. You don't suppose Peter tipped her off, do you?"

"It crossed my mind. Either way, she's like a scared rabbit now. I hope we haven't lost her for good." The light turned green and I lurched out into the intersection. Just as

I crossed, a green Volkswagen screeched to a stop on the cross street. "That's her!" I blurted, spinning the wheel to turn into a gas station on the corner.

"Take it easy," Craig said. "Don't want to let her know we're following her."

I eased into a parking space and watched her car. "She's probably lost. She's even worse than I am. I've never seen anyone spend more time going around in circles."

Her light turned green and she moved hesitantly into the intersection, as if she were debating which way to turn. I slowly backed out of the parking spot and pulled onto the road behind her.

"Okay, now just hang back a little," Craig instructed.

"I will. Just don't let me lose her."

Just as I said it, she gunned the little engine and darted in and out of traffic like an Indy racer.

"She's getting away," Craig said, peering over the dashboard to keep her in view.

I checked over my shoulder and changed lanes. I jammed my foot into the accelerator and weaved in and out of traffic to catch up to her.

"She turned right at that next street," Craig said, pointing through the windshield.

"I see her," I said, barreling around the corner after her. I kept enough distance between us that she shouldn't suspect we were following her. She seemed to be generating her own panic. Her speed kept increasing, but I hung back just enough to keep her lights in view.

"I didn't know those little cars could move that fast," Craig said. We had left the congestion of the city traffic and were on a dark, lightly-traveled road, headed south. "How fast are we going?"

I checked the speedometer. "Eighty-eight," I answered.

The road was rough and full of potholes. Up until that point, it was also straight, but something looked awry up ahead. "Slow down, Dev," Craig said, bracing himself by putting his hand on the dash.

Casey had lost her senses. She was driving like a maniac. She didn't see the curve in the road, or maybe she thought she could make it, but the laws of physics proved her wrong. From our distant view, we could see the lights of her car tumble over and over, like a wild ride at the county fair.

I skidded to a stop at the point where she left the road. Craig grabbed a flashlight and was out of the car before I could set the parking brake. There were no other cars around for miles. I ran after him, down a steep embankment to the wreck.

Craig and I struggled to get the door open. The car was upside down, and Casey hadn't taken the time to fasten her seatbelt. She looked pretty banged up, but she was alive.

"I smell gasoline," I said, as I reached in and turned the key in the ignition to the off position.

Craig handed me the flashlight. "Me too. We better get her out of here before it blows."

Casey moaned as Craig and I pulled her out of the car. We dragged her as far away as we thought was safe, then Craig began examining her injuries. Seconds later, the Volkswagen's gas tank exploded. We both jumped at the sound and cringed as the entire car was engulfed in flames.

"Casey? Can you hear me?" Craig shouted at her.

She mumbled something inaudible, but nodded her head.

"I'm a doctor, Casey. I work at San Diego General. You're gonna be okay, but we have to get you to a hospital. Do you understand?" he continued yelling.

She nodded again, then opened her mouth to speak. She had to repeat herself three times before we could understand her. "Not here," she said.

"Not here? You mean not in Mexico?" Craig pressed.

She nodded. "Get me home."

Craig and I exchanged glances. We wanted to take her back, but we hadn't counted on this. I didn't know how badly hurt she was. "What do you think?" I said.

Craig looked up the hill toward the road where our car was parked. "She's got a broken arm and probably a concussion. Possibly some internal injuries."

Casey opened her eyes and grabbed his arm. "Get me out of Mexico!" she demanded.

"Okay, okay. Calm down, Casey. We'll get you out of here," Craig assured her.

We carried her up the embankment and carefully placed her in the back seat of our car. Craig covered her with a blanket he kept in the trunk. Casey was moving in and out of consciousness.

"Casey? Can you hear me?" Craig asked her, before we closed the door. She nodded. "Keep this blanket over you until we get past the border."

She didn't speak, but I could see her nod slightly under the blanket.

Craig got behind the wheel and I took the passenger seat. When we got to the border, we were waved through without incident. Casey looked like a sleeping child in the back seat, and with her entire body covered by the blanket, her injuries went unnoticed.

I phoned Sam and told him to meet us at the hospital. We drove directly to the emergency entrance. Craig supervised the transport of Casey into the emergency room while I explained to Sam what happened. He and I sat in the waiting room until Craig came to update us on Casey's condition.

Casey's parents hurried into the waiting room just as Craig came in. "Where is she? Is she okay? What's happened?" Otis Biggsmuth blurted, not giving Craig a chance to answer.

Craig tried to calm him down. "Are you Casey's parents?" he asked.

"Yes. Yes. Is she okay?" Mrs. Biggsmuth said.

"She's going to be fine. She's got a broken arm and a concussion, but no internal injuries. She was very lucky."

Craig hadn't even finished his sentence, and Sam was gone. He was on his way to the emergency room.

Otis Biggsmuth tried to stop him. "Wait a minute! Where's he going? You tell him to leave my little girl alone!"

Craig ran after both of them, and I followed. Sam pushed his way to the gurney where Casey laid, staring at the ceiling. Otis grabbed him by the arm and knocked him down. I could see fire in Sam's eyes. He got to his feet, pointed a finger at Otis and clenched his jaw. "You do that again, and I'll cuff you to the bumper on one of those ambulances out there and drag your sorry hide to Canada and back."

Otis didn't back down. "Go ahead. I'll sue you and the entire department for—"

"Go away, Dad," Casey mumbled, loud enough to be heard.

"What did you say?" Otis demanded.

By this time, Mrs. Biggsmuth had joined the scene. Craig was trying his best to herd everyone out of the emergency room, but Sam and Otis were at a standoff.

"I said go away. I don't want you here," Casey repeated. She made a sweeping motion with her splinted arm as if to clear the entire room.

A pair of muscle-bound orderlies arrived just in time to help Craig regain control. He made everyone return to the waiting room until Casey could be transported to a private room. Everyone except Sam, who refused to let Casey out of his sight until she was in police custody. He called the station to have an officer stand guard at her room.

I wanted to avoid Otis Biggsmuth. He was as mad as a fighting bull, and I didn't want to be around if he punched a hole in something, or someone. I wandered back down the hall and around the corner to find Sam and Craig conversing. Craig waved me to join them.

"How is she?" I asked.

"She's fine, and she's under arrest," Sam answered.

"Already? But I thought—"

"It was her idea. She wouldn't stop confessing until I let Sam in to read her her rights," Craig explained.

I moved closer to Craig and squeezed his hand. "I think we might be in some kind of trouble, though. She might not have crashed if we weren't chasing her. I know her father will want to hang us out to dry."

"That's only if he knows, which I doubt he ever will," Sam assured me. "Besides, even if he does make a fuss, it's my opinion that you were a couple of good Samaritans who just happened to be driving by and saw the accident. You two saved her life."

Suddenly, I remembered Peter Champion, whom we'd left at the hotel in Tijuana. "We need to go talk to Peter to find out what happened. If he tipped her off, there's a chance that he was also involved in Lou's murder."

Sam shook his head. "He wasn't involved. She told me what happened. Did you ask him if he'd ever sailed before you came up with your plan?"

"No," I answered.

"Well, Casey has been sailing since she was four. When he showed her those pictures of your boat, she asked him a few basic questions. He didn't have a clue. That's what made her suspicious and caused her to run."

Craig put his arm around my shoulders. "The one hole in our perfect plan," he said. "We better go get your car and let Peter know what's going on."

We both looked to Sam for permission to leave. He waved us off like a pair of obedient dogs who'd performed well for houseguests.

Chapter Sixteen

Casey remained in the hospital until she was well enough to go to jail. Her father hired a team of expensive attorneys who would, no doubt, put every resource they had into getting her sentence minimized to something obscene. I wondered if those lawyers would mind if the judge released her into their custody, and they could be responsible for her actions for the rest of her life.

Sam had interrogated her several times. She confessed that she knew about Lou's fishing trip because he'd told her about it the day he bought the winning ticket. She remembered where he kept the spare key because once she had to make a grocery delivery to the house when Lou's wife was ill and Lou had to be out of town. He informed her where the key was so she could let herself in without disturbing Mrs. Winnomore.

She'd gotten the cyanide from a local chemical supply firm where one of her classmates worked part-time. She'd used what she learned from Peter Champion's art classes to come up with a formula to cover my signature on the back of the lottery ticket. She'd done a good job. It fooled the lottery officials, but now that the murder investigation was in full swing, the ticket would have to be closely inspected and put through a battery of tests. Undoubtedly, my original signature would be uncovered and a whole new can of worms would be opened.

I had to remind Sam three times that I'd won our bet. The murderer was in fact female, just as I'd predicted. He tried to weasel out, so I let him modify the payoff. He agreed to buy the food and drinks, and Craig and I took him out on the *Plan C* for a weekend fishing trip. That made it a win-win all the way around.

Bridgett Winnomore hired an attorney to help reclaim the million dollars that rightfully belonged to Lou Winnomore's heirs. In all likelihood, the money would be split equally between her son, Scotty, and Lou's two remaining children, Frankie and Nellie. Of course, Raven Covina would petition for half of Scotty's inheritance for her own son, Bahama Breeze.

Bridgett was also going to try to reclaim Arthur Simon's winnings. Even before she knew that it would be my signature found on the ticket, and not Lou Winnomore's, she insisted on naming me as a beneficiary in her lawsuit, along with her family. Gary at the King Rooster had given her a job at my recommendation, and she was so thankful, she wanted to pay me back.

Of course, there was no telling how it would all turn out. It would probably depend on who had the better lawyers. I figured Simon could afford the best, so his chances for keeping at least some of the money were pretty good. Even if he had to give it up in the end, he'd earn so much interest on it during the years that he'd probably drag it out in court that he'd still come out ahead.

I'd just put the last coat of paint on Rancho Costa Little, when Fiona barreled down the road in her big boat of a car and screeched to a halt in front of the house. I watched her pile out of the car and open the trunk. She hoisted a Fiona Oliviera Realty sign out and hung it on the post that was still planted in the ground from when I originally bought the house.

I invited her in to see how I'd fixed the place up, and to sign the sales listing.

"Oh, it's just darling, toots!" she exclaimed, as she wandered through the house, admiring the rooms. "You did such a good job."

I thanked her and we stood at the kitchen counter to go over the papers. She suggested an asking price, which was exactly what I had in mind, so the rest was easy. I signed the papers and she quickly handed me my copies and headed for the door.

"Want to celebrate? We could head over to Miguel's for a margarita," I said, as she was nearly out the door.

"Can't tonight, toots. Got a date," she said.

I raised my eyebrows. "A date? With who?"

"Arthur Simon," she answered, grinning from ear to ear, exposing that big gap between her front teeth.

"I guess you finally got his number," I said, laughing.

"I certainly do. If it works out, I'll invite you to the wedding," she said, as she gave me a wink and headed out the door.

I locked up Rancho Costa Little and headed for my car. I had to make one stop on the way home. Craig had called me earlier in the day to tell me he was taking me out to dinner. He was being very sly on the phone, so I guessed he was up to something.

I walked into the house carrying a big box wrapped with a large red ribbon and decked out with a bow. Craig greeted me at the door. He was holding an envelope, also decorated with a bow.

"Hey, yours is bigger than mine," he said, pointing at the box in my arms.

"What do you mean?" I asked, staring at the envelope in his hand.

We carried our gifts into the living room. I made Craig open his first. He was as excited about his new banjo as a kid getting his very own fire truck. He picked out a few vaguely familiar tunes and assured me that with a little practice, he'd be playing at the annual Bluegrass Festival with the pros.

I carefully opened the envelope he'd given me and pulled out the bundle of brochures. One was for Yellowstone National Park, one was for the Kentucky Derby, and the other for the Grand Ole Opry in Nashville. I smiled at him.

"The Derby is the first Saturday in May, so we need to start planning now," he said.

"Really? We're going?"

"That's just this year. Next year, we'll pick some more places we'd like to see. No point in waiting for someday. Someday never happens."

I spread the brochures out on the table in front of me

and listened to my banjo-playing husband pluck out another tune. No amount of money in the world could have made me happier than I was at that moment. I closed my eyes and wondered what I'd wear to the Derby.